THE GOLDEN HELMET

BY
RON WHITE

The Golden Helmet

Copyright © 2023 Ron White

All rights reserved. No part of this publication may be reproduced, distributed, or transmitted in any form or by any means, including photocopying, recording, or other electronic or mechanical methods, without the prior written permission of the publisher, except in the case of brief quotations embodied in critical reviews and certain other noncommercial uses permitted by copyright law.

ISBN: 978-1-960620-12-5

The Golden Helmet

TABLE OF CONTENTS

CHAPTER ONE	7
CHAPTER TWO	25
CHAPTER THREE	25
CHAPTER FOUR	46
CHAPTER FIVE	46
CHAPTER SIX	59
CHAPTER SEVEN	83
CHAPTER EIGHT	83
CHAPTER NINE	98
CHAPTER TEN	125
CHAPTER ELEVEN	125
CHAPTER TWELVE	143

The Golden Helmet

CHAPTER ONE
ONCE UPON A TIME

They say a good story always begins once upon a time and ends with and *lived happily ever after*. Well, this may well be one such story. It all started on one fine evening on August 14, 1960, in Melville, Missouri.

"Who let the *band boy in?*" someone yelled.

I stopped dead cold. I looked up.

"Did you take a wrong turn, boy?" Melville's varsity football Coach, Jim Clark, asked me forcefully.

"No, sir."

"Did you wander into the wrong barnyard?"

"No, sir. I don't think so, sir."

"What are you doing here?

"Didn't you hear it through the Melville grapevine, Coach?"

"No, hear what, Captain Paul Henri?"

"This is *Touchdown, Tommy Cameron's* little brother. His father, John-the Scott-Cameron, and his older brother, Touchdown Tommy Cameron, were both Melville football standouts?"

"Who are you?"

"They call me *Stevie Tyler Cameron, sir.*"

"Don't tell me we've got another ill-advised, goo-goo-eyed, squirrelly, no nothing, upshot, band playing, tuba toten, bugle playing, ninety-day wonder band boy with no football playing experience wanting to try out, Captain Henri? Please tell me it ain't so."

"It's so, Coach."

"But didn't he read our sign?"

"Maybe he can't read the King's English?" Captain Paul Henri stated.

"Why would he *disobey my sign*, Captain Paul Henri? *Nobody does that?*"

"Maybe his mother dropped him on his head when he was a baby?"

It wasn't their crude, obnoxious laughter, or his *no band boys need to apply* sign, or them talking about me as if I were not there that got my ire. It was the way they both said *band boy* that I objected to as if *band boy* were a dirty word. As an American citizen, I felt I had to defend my rights.

"I beg both your pardons, gentlemen, but the United States Supreme Court clearly ruled that you cannot *bar any U.S. Citizen from any public school or event without just cause.*"

"Since when?" Melville's football team Captain, Paul Henri, asked me sharply.

"Since May 17, 1954, in the historic Supreme Court case, <u>Brown vs. the Board of Education,</u> of <u>Topeka Kansas,</u> that's when. You're not allowing me to try out for this public-school varsity football team is unlawful and might cause me to have a serious and dangerous inferiority complex and could lower my tenuous self-esteem, as numerous psychological studies have shown. Read the case."

"Now look here, snarky," Mr. Clark begin. "Surely you can appreciate our need for a no admittance sign for band boys. They don't measure up. They require preferential treatment and thus lower our standards."

From weakness, I took to the offense immediately. A tactic my brother Tom had taught me early on."

Tom said:

First, you must agree with your opposition's position to disarm them. Then attack with cunning, humor, or logic.

"Yes, I can appreciate your perceived need for a no admittance sign for band boys, Mr. Clark. But most football coaches I've known wouldn't know a briefcase from a Supreme Court Case if they tripped over it."

Jim Clark struggled for an answer for only a moment and then recovered. "Well, you got me there, *band boy*. Those dim-witted assistant coaches of mine give the rest of us intelligent football coaches a bad name. Wouldn't you agree, Cameron?" He then chuckled defensively, trying to take the sting out of my poison dart.

"Yes, I do agree, just like a few provocative ill prepared band boys could give the entire Melville marching band a bad name, sir."

"Exactly," Clark said. *Checkmate,* I said to myself.

Then Captain Paul Henri chirped in, speaking fast. "Coach, you know our Melville band boys couldn't fight their way out of a wet Wheaties cereal box with a hole in it. You know that's the darn truth."

"Now, not so fast, slow down, Captain Henri. Catch your breath. You're speaking to the choir. If you can show me just one band boy, who can fight his way out of a wet Wheaties cereal box with a hole in it, I'll show you twenty band boys, who can't," Mr. Jim Clark responded.

Seizing the initiative, I replied quickly, "As for my 'not being able to fight my way out of a wet cardboard Wheaties cereal box,' gentlemen, I can happily say, I can, because I always eat my Wheaties, the breakfast of champions. Just like the famous-two time-Olympic track and field gold medalist winner, Bob Richards, who proudly proclaimed:

> *You can do it, don't give up.*
> *In America, your dream can come true,*
> *And God will help you."*

Clark reacted quickly in turn. "Well, that can-do speech was damn inspiring, Cameron. I loved it. I truly did. And it came at us right out of the blue. I especially liked that parable and how you brought Bob Richards-that Olympic pole vaulter-the *Vaulting Vicar,* into your comparison. The first athlete ever to have his picture plastered on a Wheaties cereal box, the *pole-vaulting Parson*, they also called him. That was a particularly nice touch. All though I thought for certain you would choose Superman as your comparison seeing how you are dressed like Jim Dandy today. But you must know why we don't allow band boys to try out for our football team. It's nothing personal. Any further questions before we dismiss him, Captain Henri?"

"Yeah, coach, I have one more thing, if I may, for the honorable Stevie Tyler Cameron."

Captain Henri proceeded to question me like our senate congressional committee members questioned those they suspected of being communists. "Did you or did you not *read the no admittance sign* for *band boys* that hangs above the varsity football locker room door?" Captain Paul Henri asked me bluntly.

"Of course, I read that disgusting, discriminating sign, Captain Henri."

"But you entered anyway?"

"Yes, of course, I entered anyway."

"Why?"

"It was the entrance."

Jim Clark held a smile and a twinkle in both his eyes. I continued. "My father, *John Cameron*, and many years later, my brother, *Tom Cameron*, were both Melville *band boys* who were barred from *attending junior varsity tryouts*, Mr. Clark. You laughed and sent them packing, Mr. Clark, and told them to be more realistic and not to bother coming back until they grew taller, could run faster, and tackle harder. Well, they came back bigger, faster, and could tackle harder. No one is laughing anymore."

"Yes, as I recall, they were *both inappropriately, nauseatingly provocative,*" Clark said, remembering. "But they were the exception, you know. They matured physically, mentally, and emotionally and the rest is like what our Melville Times sports writer, Bret Hart, says when closing his radio broadcast: *and that, folks, is Melville sports history*. But thanks for that little dab of football history, Cameron. That jogged my memory like a cool blast from the past, as for the Melville band boys. I've found, *a little dab will do ya,*" Jim Clark stated, quoting an advertisement jingle from Brylcream, a popular men's hair grooming product. All nine of the football veterans laughed hardily. So, tell me again why you are here, boy?" Jim Clark asked me.

"I'm on a *mission, sir, not entirely of my own choosing.*"

"Oh, well then, it's ok, Coach, relax; *he's on a mission not totally of his own choosing,*" Captain Henri mocked.

But Clark reacted forcefully. He quickly pointed to the locker room door. The very one I had entered. I turned and started to walk toward that exit door when...

"Wait...stop. Hold up a minute. Don't go away mad, Cameron," Captain Paul Henri said.

So, I stopped, and I waited. Captain Henri's eyes danced with me fast, then his voice drifted off slow like a Tennessee waltz. "I think I like this rule breaker, Coach."

"What, why?"

"He has spunk."

"I hate spunk. It borders on disobedience and is usually followed by arrogance. There is a fine line between spunk and overconfidence and arrogance. So, tell me, why are you hesitating now, Captain Henri?"

"I'm intrigued."

"You're intrigued?"

"Yes, he's different."

"Yes, he's different, all right. But being different can be dangerous. Don't tell me now you're going to plead for his admittance Captain Henri?" Clark asked, looking concerned. "I'll bet your house is full of stray cats and dogs you don't have room for and can't afford to feed. Am I right, Captain Henri?"

"Yes, you know I do have a few, Coach. But there is always room for one more."

"Well, get to it. But don't let your kind heart and keen mind cloud your judgment, Captain Henri. We draw a tight, bright red line here for a very good reason. Do you have an unanswered question?"

"Yes, I have three more things to ask Cameron before we let him go?"

"Like what?"

"Like, why did he quit the Melville marching band? Why is he trying out for our football team as a senior? Why is he wearing that Superman t-shirt? Why is he carrying that old torn blue gym bag? What is his mission if it is not of his own choosing? Don't you have an inquiring mind, Coach? Don't you read the tabloids like The National Enquirer?"

"Some day's yes and some day's no, Captain Henri. Ok, all right, take your time and interrogate him further, Captain Henri; ask your probing questions, find out what you will, but hurry. You know those pesky no-nothing underclassmen will soon be charging in here any minute wanting this and asking for that getting ready *for the fun run* and *Clark's hell,* as our resident Melville sports writer, Bret Hart, calls it. Personally, I sometimes think Bret Hart spends more time hanging out here bothering me than he does working at his job at the Melville Times News as a sports writer and a sportscaster at the local radio station," Clark pointed.

"Won't Bret Hart be here later, Coach?" Captain Henri asked. His voice rising.

"Henri, you know ole Bret Hart never misses the first day of *Clark's Hell*. He believes the long endurance march separates the men from the boys," Clark shared.

"Melville's young boys-eager to make this team-would walk on hot coals if asked to, Coach," Captain Henri stated. Clark smiled.

Paul Henri, the boy with the square-jawed disposition, moved toward me. Henri placed one foot and then the other upon it on a wooden bench. He methodically tied his white tennis shoe laces, making me all the more nervous. Not knowing what to expect, I waited silently. When Paul Henri finished tying his tennis shoe laces, he stood upright, turned and faced me, and said this with conviction,

"Band boy, you do have a plan?"

"Yes, I have a plan, of course. Do you want to hear it now, Captain Henri?"

"Yes, of course. But get to the point."

"Well, ok, first, I'll memorize all your offensive plays and then all your defensive formations. After two weeks, if all goes well, I'll become your starting quarterback and remove your present quarterback, Bobby Hanuman and alternate him at right halfback so he won't get hurt. He loves to run, so let him."

"Really, that's your plan, Cameron? Move our star quarterback to the right half, really?" Henri asked, appearing unimpressed.

"God willing, yes, I would move him from quarterback to right halfback."

"And you would do this position change because Bobby's weaknesses at quarterback are?"

"Bobby's weaknesses at quarterback are three-fold, Captain Henri. First, Bobby can't pass the football on the run."

"Ok, all right, and second?"

"And second, if he did run, he couldn't hit a bull in the ass with a handful of pumpkins." At that, everyone laughed.

"And third?"

"And third, he likes to toy with the other team's defense too much, probably because he is an excellent broken-field runner, and he can. He needs to stay in the protective pocket more and run as a last resort."

"And fourth?"

"There is no fourth."

"What else, Cameron? What other changes would you make to our team? Don't hold back. Who else would you move to another position?"

"I would move you, Captain Henri."

"What?! Me. Move me? Where to? The peanut gallery?" Most of everyone laughed again but not as loud.

"No, I would move you from your strong right defensive right guard position to defensive linebacker. You're an aggressive player who loves contact, right? I would call you the monster man. From the linebacker position, you could control the whole interior of the defensive line from end to end rather than the right tackle slot where you now reign supreme. Sure, you're the team's captain, but that title is an empty vase. Your talent and skill must be put to better use, Captain Henri, as a linebacker. We Germans are a meticulous bunch, you know."

Clark chuckled. "Henri, what do you think now? Are you sorry you opened this Pandora's Box?"

"I must say I do like that idea of my being a linebacker, Coach. I believe he has something there. Me controlling the whole line from end-to-end sounds like an incredible challenge and lots of fun." When Henri smiled reassuringly at me, I felt I had moved Henri closer to my side until he said, "But one more thing, Coach, if I might?"

"Sure, go ahead, Henri. He's all yours. Grill him!"

I wanted their pointed questions to end. I wondered if I could take The Fifth Amendment on the grounds it may incriminate me like Jimmy Hoffa did and the mafia-wise guys did.

"Cameron, what makes you know our football team so well?" Captain Henri asked.

"From my stadium seat on the fifty-yard line, I can see clearly. I have been a member of the Melville marching band for five years now with perfect game attendance. I have seen fifty Melville football games counting home and away. Remember, the Melville band travels by Grey Hound bus to every football game. In addition, anywhere ever I go in Melville, the football fans talk Melville football. They talk the A B C of it. They talk about the good ole days when they played or someone they know played. They talk about the coaches, the assistant coaches, and the star players from the opponent's teams with reverence and respect. They compare, and they contrast. They know all their season records. They compare players and recite statistics so accurate one might think they were reading from a Topps' bubble gum card. Then, in addition, my brother Tom and his football friends continuously talk Melville football." I sighed deeply. "Melville football has a language all its own. *Fade-ins and fade-outs, right 27 go, 46 Wahoo, etc.* And finally, Bret Hart discusses and writes about your Melville football program in his sports column and radio sports show daily. There is no escaping Melville football if you live in Melville like I do. Believe me, I've tried. Melville football is a holy affair around here."

"If you don't love it, you wouldn't understand it, Cameron," Captain Henri stated, making a strong point.

"Bobby, how do you like being moved out of your starting quarterback position by a *band boy* and a few veteran football players from the distant past? And did you like being told you couldn't throw on the run, and if you did, you couldn't hit a bull in the ass with a handful of pumpkins," Clark asked.

"Cameron's right, Coach. I can't throw the football on the run. I get all discombobulated. But I do love to carry the football and toy with the opponent's defenses. I do love that." Bobby chuckled at the thought. "It's like I'm playing a game I call; *catch me if you can*, like we do on the sand lots and the playgrounds and over at Bo Howards Beach."

"Then you agree with a damn band, boy?"

"Well, yes, I would love to be a halfback again like I was in the Pop Warner League and pee-wee league and run with the football more,' Bobby shared, remembering fondly.

Not hearing the answer, he wanted, Clark turned toward me quickly. He tried a different approach. "So, you're asking us to believe you showed up here today at my house, at my door, and you *expect instant success*? Do you really expect to make this team at quarterback, Cameron, with no experience, really?"

"Well, yes, of course. I certainly do, Mr. Clark. Nothing good comes about when thinking negative, now does it? Like my brother, *Touchdown Tommy*, always says:

"If you play with the talent you're given,

And all the self-confidence you can muster,
Success will surely follow."

Coach Clark paused for a bit, trying to collect his words before finally speaking,

"You talk like you expect instant success like you're fixing an early morning omelet or fixing a cup of Sanka's instant coffee or something."

"Indeed, Mr. Clark. "I have <u>great expectations,</u> like Pip, metaphorically speaking, of course."

"Who the hell is Pip? Clark asked. "And what is metaphorically speaking?"

I quickly explained to Mr. Clark that Pip was the lead character in the great Charles Dickens' classical literary novel, Great Expectations. But trying to explain what a metaphor was became more challenging.

"Who talks like this, Captain Henri? Tell me quick. Who is it?"

"Daffy Duck, Goofy," Captain Henri yelled out quickly, using Disney cartoon characters as his comparisons. All the veterans laughed out loud at my expense, again not holding me in high esteem. "Wait, I'm thinking, um… Give me a minute, Coach..." Henri said, searching the recesses of his mind.

"So, which *one of these three goals* have you planned for an encore, Cameron?" Clark asked me with a jaundiced eye. "Metaphorically speaking?" he added. "Winning the Missouri

Valley Athletic League Conference and helping us have an undefeated season? Winning the Golden Helmet because of having Great *expectations,* like *Pip?"*

"All of them!" I replied.

"That's it! Captain Henri, call the State's Lunatic Asylum in Vernon County and have this band boy committed to the State's Lunatic Asylum. He's out of his damn mind."

"I think they tore that old asylum down, Coach Clark," Captain Henri stated.

Clark's eyes squinted. "That won't matter, Henri, because I'm going to strangle him myself."

Captain Henri held him back. "I can't understand why you recite these snappy slick insipid platitudes and parables, Cameron. Surely you don't expect to waltz in here and move my players about like pieces on a chessboard. Then make our first team, as a junior, mind you. Then become our starting quarterback and win our most prized athletic award, the Golden Helmet, simply because you showed up here having Great Expectations, like Pip and High Hope's, like Frank Sinatra's hit song?"

"Well, yes, that's exactly my intended purpose. I love the sheer determination of that little ole ant. Who sets about moving that rubber tree plant? When anyone knows an ant, can't?"

As a musician, I could mentally hear Frank Sinatra singing these lyrics from his 1959 song, High Hopes:

Next time you're found with your chin on the ground

There is a lot to be learned, so look around

Just what makes that little old ant

Think he'll move that rubber tree plant

Anyone knows an ant can't

Move a rubber tree plant

But he's got high hopes

He's got high hopes,

He's got high apple pie, in the sky hopes.

In 1960, Frank Sinatra's popular hit song, High Hopes, won an Oscar for Best Original Song at the 32nd Hollywood Academy Awards. I learned to play that song on several instruments and could sing the words for the fun of it and for motivation.

"But what makes you think we need your help, Cameron? Our team's record is pretty impressive, no brag, just facts," Coach Clark boasted, and rightfully so.

"Yes, Mr. Clark, your team's record is impressive. That's a fact. But you have one catastrophic problem."

"What catastrophic problem?" Clark asked quickly and defensively, his eyebrows now raised.

"You can't close the big game. This has to be embarrassing for you as the Head Coach? Last year, Centerville's new Head Coach,

Gary Thorn, ate your lunch. It seems you can't defeat Thorn and his Centerville's thugs."

"What makes you think you know so much?"

"I read Bret Harts' sports column often. We listen every evening around supper time to Bret's radio sports show. My grandmother is a big fan. She records every show and plays them back while cooking. Now according to Bret Hart, Thorn's goal is simple: Destroy Melville! Yet, your coaching philosophy remains the same. Win the Missouri Valley Athletic league championship first. Go undefeated second. Then, on Thanksgiving, *defeat* your *arch-rival,* Centerville, handedly, on Turkey Day and go home. Have you never considered that maybe your Melville football program goals are too broad, Mr. Clark? About three months ago, I read where our U.S. Navy penned this acronym, KISS, which means: Keep it simple stupid."

Clark weighed in quickly, his voice strong and not surprisingly defensive. "Stupid, huh? Why that is the most simplistic description of Melville football coaching I've ever heard. If only it were that simple, Cameron. Win a championship! Go undefeated. Defeat Centerville handedly and go home."

"I believe a positive attitude defeats negative thinking every time, Mr. Clark, don't you?"

"Confidence has its place," Clark commented. "But I worry about overconfidence and then becoming arrogant," he added. "Then you risk becoming careless and sloppy."

Captain Henri had a twinkle in both his eyes in anticipation of what he was about to say next.

CHAPTER TWO
I GET NO RESPECT

"You forgot 'and live happily ever after,' Coach," Captain Henri said, being very smug and sarcastic once again. "That's important."

"Yeah, that's important; fat chance on that happening, right, Captain Henri?" Coach Clark said, with a smirk on his face.

"Yeah, who lives happily ever after, Coach?"

Coach Clark, now with a more serious expression, began, "Cameron, your analysis is bone-chilling, arrogant, and condescending. First, no one likes to be called stupid, and second, no one is going to remember that silly KISS slogan either. That won't catch on. It will fizzle out. Only one person I know has your simplistic view of football, and his name is Gary Lee Thorn. The very coach you referenced. Thorn - whose last name is appropriate - believes Centerville's football season is only successful if they defeat us. Why can he lose every game on his tough ten-game football schedule, but if he defeats or ties us, his season is considered a success? Go figure. And what makes it worse, almost everyone in Centerville agrees with him. Whereas we, on the other hand, as you have pointed out, want to win every game, remain undefeated, then go home and live happily ever after like you say, but with a little more pride in our step and a larger feeling of accomplishment knowing we followed and played by the rules."

"Playing by the rules in football and in life is important. Thorn is a rule breaker, a renegade. He never met a rule he wouldn't break. He will stoop to a very low level, something we can't compete with."

"There is more to this Melville football program than winning all ten games on the football schedule, like you say, Cameron. But what is so wrong about winning all ten of our season's games on the field of battle fairly and winning the Missouri Valley Athletic League championship, too, if we can, I ask?

"Well, that answer is obvious. Your broad athletic goal is simply more ambitious than Mr. Gary Thorns and is, therefore, more difficult to achieve. You have two different approaches going forward. On the other hand, Mr. Thorn's goal is simpler, more narrowly focused, and therefore has a much better chance of success. Why not put all your effort into winning one war, like your ex-friend and assistant coach Gary Thorn does? Not all ten at the same time; it prevents you from focusing on just one thing."

Clark reacted angrily. "Look, I'm not here to criticize your plan as you have criticized mine."

"But you must admit you to have Great Expectations and High Hopes, Mr. Clark."

Clark's annoyance was palpable now.

"Henri, I think I'm learning to dislike this band boy the longer I know him. Don't let me strangle him. I'm too close to retirement, and I know the board of education would frown heavily on that. My enemies in high places are just waiting for me to commit some big infraction so they can take me out. Those bastards!"

"Should we remind Cameron yours is an authoritarian dictatorship you have here and unless he wants to sue us, we will ignore the Supreme Court's 1954 decision?" Captain Henri asked, thinking he had found the permanent solution.

"Look, I do not wish to discuss my team's goals or Gary Thorn's goals with you, a junior band boy, but I will say this: neither you nor Gary Thorn is my friend. Honestly, I find a little bit of you and Gary Thorn goes a long way. I hired him; I fired him. I hired him again. And that last hire was the worst mistake I've ever made, which I will make sure to not repeat."

Listening to him talk, I just wanted to correct Mr. Clark on one point where he referred to me twice as a junior band boy when in fact, I was not. I was a senior band boy. A minor point, at best, that could and should be discussed later.

"Look, I don't mean to rain on your New York Lindbergh ticker tape parade or slam you to the ground and pin you down, Cameron. I like a boy with a big dream, high hopes, and great expectations, like Pip. I really do. And yes, I, too, dream big. But we don't admit band boys into our varsity football program for two very good reasons."

"Because they can't walk and chew gum at the same time." Paul Henri said, interrupting Clark in an attempt to be funny—all the seated veterans laughed.

Clark smiled lightly, then chuckled lightly, then recovered and continued, "But seriously, Cameron, you must agree, football is a demanding and dangerous blood sport. Everyone knows most band boys are not coordinated or aggressive enough to play this game. Not everyone shares in the splendor and glory of our football program, and for that, we are sorry. This aggressive, rugged, American game we call football is not for the dreamers, walk-ons, weak of heart, or fun-loving minstrels like yourself, Cameron."

Captain Henri added, "Some teams get nervous when we run onto the field, as well they should. The name Melville alone causes shivers in our adversary's hearts because this is where all four Kelly Springfield all-weather radial white-wall tires meet the Missouri asphalt. Maybe you haven't noticed Cameron, having seen fifty of our games. But this is not a pick-up, intramural, or flag football program Coach Clark is running here where everyone who shows is given a chance to play and have a swell ole time. This is Melville football where the tough and the motivated only need apply, not minstrels, clowns, and band boys."

"But as long as we have a few good men who are willing to sacrifice for so many, America will survive. And when that happens, it is quite extraordinary to see. It warms my heart," Clark said.

"But by you showing up here today, late, with no football playing experience makes a powerful statement. It says anyone can play Melville football, even an inexperienced band boy like yourself. Now, I don't believe that for a minute and can't understand why you do," Jim Clark added.

"Coach is right; most all the athletes seated here have been playing some form of football since they were babies, so you know they're a different league altogether."

I took a deep breath, trying to glean what I could from Captain Henri's and Mr. Clarks' comments, when Captain Henri said, "All he is saying, Cameron, maybe you should give us and this Melville football program a little respect."

I remembered what the fidgeting stand-up comedian Rodney Dangerfield said regarding respect:

I get no respect

"Coach, I've been thinking…" Captain Henri began.

"Hell, now that can be dangerous," Clark remarked.

"We are two nice guys, and we have our share of critics and second guessers and Monday morning quarterbacks."

"Yes, of course, so?"

"Yes, well, Maybe Cameron is just another plain ole, naïve senior Milo Clem band boy who made some promises and set some goals he can't possibly keep or achieve. We all do that, sometimes. We can't blame Cameron for that. Everyone is envious of those of us who carry the mail. Everyone would love to be a Melville football hero. Those who can't play are jealous and join the band or the chess club. It's normal. But most of these seniors you see seated here have been paid their dues. For that, they do deserve our respect. But does that mean we have to exclude Cameron, Coach? I say maybe we need to have a bigger tent and be more inclusive. Remember, you have a no-cut policy, Coach."

"Yes, well, you've got me there, Captain Henri. I do respect inclusivity, so what do you suggest we do?"

"I think we should not send him home right away. For now, let's tear down the signs that say "illegal." For that, we don't need a permission slip, only a new policy. A policy that says we're more inclusive," Captain Henri shrugged.

"You're saying we do not need this controversy, and it can be avoided if we allow this provocative band boy and the others like him to try out for our football team anytime, they please?" Clark confirmed as if he didn't understand it the first time.

He then began, "You want me to eliminate years of tradition and honored values in the name of diversity. Do you want to cheapen what it takes years to become a Melville man? I just won't have it.

A man has to stand for something, or he will lose everything. Inclusivity and diversity are all the words that sound good, but in reality, we have to maintain our credibility, and that won't happen if you find every other Junior Boyband a part of the Melville."

I determined now might not be a good time to tell Clark and Captain Henri I planned to write a literary young adult fiction novel about my Melville football experience.

"Let the program do the cutting, Coach." Captain Henri said. "That's all I'm asking." Then Captain Henri chuckled mischievously. The kind of chuckle that I knew spelled trouble for me with a capital T.

Jim Clark let out a deep sigh. "Tell me again why I should let him stay?"

Clark quickly turned toward Captain Henri once again. Their eyes locked. "Is he the football club's new flavor of the month, Henri? Is that it? Is that why you are supporting him?"

"He says he wants to be our quarterback, bring back the glory years, and win Melville's most prestigious award, The Golden Helmet. Like his father and brother Tom. Put simply, they hope he plays half as well as his father John Cameron and brother Tom did." Henri said.

Clark sighed. "If they think this Cameron will be our savior this year, the Football Club and Booster Club boys may be holding a bag full of empty hopes, metaphorically speaking," Clark said, glancing at me. "I know, I know, Henri. Not pleasing the Melville football club is never politically wise. They will support me one day and be my worst enemy the next."

"It depends upon which side of the street they wake up on and whether or not we are winning." Captain Henri said. "You know, no one in the football club or the booster club has any true allegiance to our athletes or coaches when we lose. They only love a winner."

"You can't count on them, Captain Henri. They are a fickle bunch. But don't quote me on that and get me into more trouble with them. If any of you boys quote me on that, I will call you a damn liar," Clark announced.

"Ok, don't dance around the edges, Henri. Tell me, do the football and booster club fellows really like Cameron? If so, what do they see in him that I don't?"

"Well, they like his spirit, his confidence, and his keen perceptions. They say they like his stated commitment and his drive to actually lead us to a win. I say let him stay because, at the very least, the chances of Cameron surviving-just today alone-are slim and slimmer and probably none. We must leverage his enthusiasm and not walk away from him for that.

This team could use an infusion of new blood and a fresh perspective, if only for one day. Everyone has the right to try out and the right to fail. Let's give Cameron his chance at fame and glory and his chance to fail. Don't leave him dangling, or they will blame you and your rigid old-school policy. We need to find out what inspires him and what drives his actions. But hear me now. He will fail. Almost everyone who tries out fresh fails. Look around you. What do you see, nothing but seasoned veterans for one good reason? It takes years to become a Melville Man."

"You're saying he won't last through today, huh," Clark said, pondering.

"Exactly, yes, that is his challenge. What's life without a good challenge to try men's souls, Coach?" Once again, Henri smiled devilishly.

"Hmm, this is a very hard sale for me, Captain Henri. I'll have to hold my nose and swallow hard like I do that God awful Geritol tonic my wife gives me for tired blood. But don't downplay his needs, of which there are many. This could be a bad news story from the get-go." Clark said.

"Yes, but this could also be a good news story if he learns this sport fast and if he has the right stuff. At the very least, we can always use him as a tackling dummy. We always need a good live dummy holder and someone to carry those heavy tan tackling dummies in and out to practice," Henri explained cleverly.

"If, if, if, and what if?" Jim Clark said, rumbling forward, talking as he walked. "Captain Henri, are you willing to take charge of this young green aspiring band boy who is already plucking my nerves, and will you will personally be responsible for him and keep him in line? Can you promise me that? I don't have time to wet nurse another band boy."

Paul Henri shook his head instantly; he couldn't believe it was finally an almost "yes," and I knew then I had a feeble chance of getting in.

"Tell me again why I should let him stay?" Clark asked with a raise eye brow, scrutinizing me.

"You know you love a good challenge, Coach," Captain Henri replied, leaving Clark with a slight smirk on his face.

CHAPTER THREE
I MADE PROMISES

While Jim Clark appraised my athletic readiness, I quickly appraised his physique, attire, and motivation. Everyone has seen a version of this old high school Coach. The look of an athlete permeated his being. Clark's Popeye-like biceps reminded me of what that old Scottish master of dialogue, the writer and poet Sir Walter Scott, once wrote:

For hardy sports or contests, bold,

His limbs were cast in manly mode.

You could see someone like Clark in every high school yearbook across America. Jim Clark stood six feet tall. He had short black hair, a thick neck, a warm, intense suntanned face, an uplifted chest, and large biceps. He wore a baseball cap, T-shirt, and a thin black belt. He had freshly polished black football shoes, white shoe laces sweat socks pulled up evenly. What caught my eye the most, the golden whistle that hung about his neck on a gold chain? I sensed Jim Clark had pride, a strong ego, and a ton of conviction. So much so that I expected to see him levitate at any moment or even walk on water or die and rise again from the dead. But after more careful scrutiny and by mere speculation, if Coach Jim Clark did walk on water, it would have to be at low tide.

I often wondered why Jim Clark coached. What was in it for him? Did football hold the heroic experience he craved? You could flip through any Old Melville yearbook or any of the old football programs and find his iconic Norman Rockwell-like picture there. But what did Clark seek: Adventure, excitement, glory, or the generic answer Clark always gave when interviewed by Melville sports writer Bret Hart?

The world is scary, and there is always someone in it. Bret, Who wants what we have or wants to take it away?

Later, when I told my friend Lax Exley this, he said: "I don't buy that malarkey for a minute. I believe Jim Clark coaches football for two reasons. The case closed to gain name recognition and get some ink for his achievements."

I remembered what the psychologist Abraham Maslow said about man's motivations:

Man's motivations by actions are toward goal attainment and esteem.

"So, you think it's all about him reaching his goals, feeding his ego and his self-esteem, and no worry or concern about the defense of our country?"

"Absolutely, positively, case closed," Lax replied.

"So why do you play football, Lax?"

"Bottom line, you want the bottom line, Natural?"

"Yes, of course."

"I only play football for one reason: to make a hit with the girls." It was no secret Melville's school girls happily pursued Melville football players in a fever hotter than a red peppers snout.

"Case closed, Lax?"

"Yes, case closed, Natural?"

But I thought Lax played football to gain validation, escape our small-town boredom, and meet a deep-seated need to be loved and appreciated. Therefore, playing football, I thought, should help Lax meet his need to be loved. Likewise, Jim Clark could obtain his self-esteem needs by having an undefeated season and by winning the Missouri Valley Athletic League championship. Coaches like Jim Clark need to win football games to satisfy their egos.

Clark turned to face me and asked me this. "Are you a plain, naïve senior band boy like Captain Henri says, Cameron?"

"Well, yes, my Grandmother Helmick-on my mother's side-says I'm very naïve, for my seventeen years on God's green earth. She says I'm an idealist, an optimist, and a hopeless romantic who looks at life through cherry-colored glasses and believes everything will turn out okay if you believe in yourself, your destiny, and an almighty God."

"Well, I'm a realist, Cameron, not an idealist, and I'm certainly not a romantic or a pessimist. But I believe if things can get worse, they will. I go to church and believe in God, but I'm not naïve, nor do I believe in destiny or luck. I believe we make our own destiny and our own luck, the fashionable way, we earn it. I don't speak out impulsively. I think through my every action. The truth is while you may trust everyone. I trust no one. My wife and her family call me paranoid. Go figure. Now, as for my strong belief in a God, well, I found in the war when the artillery shells were in coming, there were not many atheists in my fox hole. What do you think about that, Cameron?"

"Well, even an atheist gets it right sometimes."

"Any more questions for Cameron, Henri, before we let him go?"

"Yes, I need to ask Cameron one more thing, Coach, if I May?"

"Sure, shoot, Captain Henri. "The floor is yours."

Captain Henri stepped closer. Too close. He made me feel uncomfortable. He looked me straight in the face. "Could you join this veteran Melville football team tighter than a Siamese twin, Cameron?" His question hung in the stale air of his stuffy Melville football locker room like a skunk's foul spray. Captain Paul Henri, Jim Clark, and all the senior veterans seated stared at me hard and waited to hear my response.

"May I ask you a question first, Mr. Henri?" I said.

"Yeah, Mr. Cameron, shoot."

"Are you asking me if I could commit to this Melville varsity football program and these varsity players seated here completely and solemnly? Is that your question?" I knew what he wanted to hear me say. But I had no such conviction. I held no such beliefs. Putting it bluntly, I did not respect these boys.

"Yes, can you join this team tighter than a Siamese twin?"

"No, Captain Henri. No, I can't see myself joined at the hip tighter than a Siamese twin with these ruffians, who treat us, band boys, as if we were a fresh can of yellow play dough to be squeezed, punched, choked, slapped, and tossed about for their entertainment and sport! But I made promises.

Without warning, this rugged 67-year-old coach swept across the old gray cement locker room floor toward me. "Whoa. Say that last part again, son. I couldn't hear you, but I'm closer now." Clark forced his closely shaven face-which smell of Mennen after shave-up tight in mine. We stood eye ball to eye ball temple to temple. "Don't hold back now. Say that last part again, Cameron. Don't hold that loaded pistol-with the hair trigger-to my temple unless you intend to fire it." Clark said.

"I, I made promises?"

"Yes, yes, that part. Now go on."

"I made promises that I would never quit, Sir.

"Never quit, Cameron?" Clark chuckled.

"No, never!"

Jim Clark stepped back sharply. He wore a peculiar cold puppet-like smile and cocked his head slightly. With that single disbelieving glance, he protested. He purposely pushed his tongue solidly against the inside of his left cheek in false politeness. I had never seen any adult do this or act so rude. I felt belittled. I wondered where Jim Clark learned such disquieting behavior. My usual, happily confident self-esteem received a sharp smack down. Body language can hurt as much as strong words. It didn't take long for any friendship we might have developed to fizzle. I didn't feel the love. I feared our relationship, from this point forward, would be adversarial. Obviously a lose-lose for me. However, I felt that if I understood Jim Clark's motivations, it might serve me well. I wondered what made him want to degrade, emasculate, and belittle Melville band boys so. Did his self-esteem feel threatened? While my mind searched for answers, I questioned my own actions. Had I challenged his leadership and authority by speaking out? He couldn't stand for that. No leader would have. He had to have the last word and let me, as well as every senior tryout present, know who was in charge. I sensed Clark would only allow one man to stand in the spotlight. That one man was he.

"Is there a problem here, Mr. Clark?"

"Yes, a serious problem. I fear your promises are like most New Years' Resolutions, Cameron. They are made easily and dropped easily, and rarely kept. I've seen many good men on Bataan-in the Philippines and on the Bataan Death March make promises they couldn't keep. Write checks that their bodies and souls could not cash while fighting fatigue, dysentery, and malnutrition. Some gave their all, their last full measure of devotion. Others marched as far as they could until they dropped. The rest, tired, thirsty, and sick, marched on bravely. When we marched to the death camp, O'Donnell, I swore then that if I survived, if I made it through that long degrading death march and made it out of that Hellish death camp, O'Donnell, I would see to it-the youth of Melville-would be better prepared for a war than we were. I, too, aim to keep my promise, Cameron. But time wears away at my conviction the more I see of this next generation. I wonder if your generation has the right stuff. The stuff my generation had."

I had heard all those heroic tales of Jim Clark's Melville's football program where players under his tutelage were transformed from mediocrity into formidable football warriors who were better prepared for the war than life. I wanted; no, I needed this metamorphosis to succeed and accomplish my mission.

"Can we trust him if this were a combat situation, Captain Henri?"

"Well, his showing up late on our first day of tryouts does not bode well. That tells us three things about him, Coach. He is unreliable, irresponsible, and undependable too. In combat, every man's life depends on his brothers covering his back. Trust is what builds that bond." Henri said.

For a moment, I thought Captain Henri was quoting from another Frank Sinatra song.

"Captain Henri, can we be certain he will never cut and run at first sight of blood or after his first good dog fight?"

Captain Paul Henri's penetrating eyes appraised me once again like no one had done before. I felt unsettled. "In a combat situation would I trust Cameron to cover my back, hmm, that is the premier question, isn't it, Coach?"

"Indeed."

"Well, the fact that he came here late today would make me question his trustworthiness, Coach. But one thing is certain. When this green band boy faces the kind of live music you play, he will crumble faster than Mr. Saperstein's week-old, third-shelf, bakery store peanut butter cookies. Yes, he'll quit. Yes, he'll surrender. Yes, he'll cut and run. Like the British retreated in 1812 at The Battle of New Orleans." Captain Paul Henri and his best friend and right tackle Big John Mc Kinney-with a gleam in their eyes-stood and broke into song like two happily drunken sailors. Together they sang the fifth stanza of Jhonny Horton's 1959 popular country song-Battle of New Orleans.

Yeah, they ran through the briars, and they ran through the brambles
And they ran through the bushes where a rabbit couldn't go
They ran so fast that the hounds couldn't catch' em,
Down the Mississippi to the Gulf of Mexico.

"Hey." They yelled. The two veterans-who were obviously close friends-were not that bad as harmonizers despite singing with a mid-west nasal twang. Nevertheless, everyone clapped, and they sat down smiling.

"You boys sing very well together, Captain Henri. Maybe you should be on the stage." Clark said sincerely.

"Yeah, there is one leaving in five minutes." Melville's quarterback Bobby Hanuman shouted. Everyone laughed enthusiastically. Henri's face turned beet red, embarrassed, then hurt, then angry. I quickly realized the funny thing about personal humor is it can create an ill will when begotten at someone else's expense. I also realized this team had dissension, as I suspected.

"Why act so nasty, Bobby?" A hurt Captain Henri asked Bobby Hanuman.

"PMS," Melville's tall right tackle, Big John McKinney, shouted out, and all the veterans now laughed at quarterback Bobby Hanumans' expense. I remembered what my brother Tom once said about making a joke at someone else's expense:

Stevie never makes a joke at someone else's expense, especially in public. It cheapens them, and it cheapens you.

And you never kick a junkyard dog. He may turn and bite you. While I enjoyed the spontaneity Captain Paul Henri and Big John possessed. Jim Clark had another agenda. "Cameron, when you're down and your back is against the wall, will you never give in, never, never, never? Can you make me believe that?"

I instantly recalled Prime Minister Winston Churchill's fiery speech delivered in his peculiar strong raspy voice to the Parliament of the United Kingdom on June 4, 1940, when England was in a total war of national survival and the Second World Wars outcome was questionable:

We shall not flag or fail. We shall go on to the end. We shall fight in France; we shall fight on the seas and oceans. We shall fight with growing confidence and growing strength in the air. We shall defend our Island, whatever the cost may be. We will fight on the beaches. We shall fight on the landing grounds. We shall fight in the fields and in the streets. We shall fight in the hills; we shall never surrender.

"Is that all you want to know? This is your core fear, Mr. Clark? Do I have the right stuff?"

"Yes, that is the question I ask every want-to-be Melville High School football player on day one. Will you never surrender? Will you go on to the end when all others fail?" Jim Clark asked me passionately.

"No, I won't ever surrender. I promise."

"I've heard all those bold promises before, Cameron. Our General, Edward P. King, disobeyed a no surrender order on Bataan. He thought his men were too weak to carry on the fight. He made a command decision. Now, I see your lips are moving just as he did. And your tongue is wagging just like his, but fast talk is cheap. And cheap talk is even cheaper. You're saying the right words, Snarky. But will you never surrender?"

"Sir, I said, I will not give in. I will never surrender. No, I will never give up."

"You will never give up, huh? Of this, we can be certain, Cameron."

Tiring of Clark's insistence, I said. "Yes, of course, Mr. Clark. You can take that bold promise to the Bedford Falls Savings and Loan bank. But if you want a loan, you must make sure you talk to George Bailey and not Mr. Potter?"

"What? Who? You talk strangely. Who are you, Cameron?"

CHAPTER FOUR
A CENTERVILLE SPY

"Ah, *nobody*, I guess." "*Nobody*, huh? Now that's another interesting answer right there. We get midnight phone calls at the house. When I ask my wife, Connie, who called, she says: *nobody* called, dear. Well, *somebody* damn sure called. Are you that *somebody,* Cameron? Did you make those late Friday night phone calls to my house and sing those fight songs to my wife?"

But being nervous, I answered incorrectly. "Yes, sir."

"What?"

"I mean, no, sir. I mean, well, maybe it's the wrong number. Are you on a party line, Mr. Clark? I hear they can be very annoying?"

It was at that instant my mind and memory couldn't agree. I felt a cold chill.

"How can we be sure it is not you yanking on my chain, Cameron?"

"Well, we can't be certain of anything but paying taxes and death, Sir. But we can't afford a telephone, you know, and I'm not going to waste a dime on a pay phone, that's for sure. Like my grandmother Helmick says, we're so *poor* the church mice moved out. Sometimes she can be so funny. Isn't she a gas? Anyway, I hate those close tight little phone booths with the swinging doors."

"Why?"

"I'm very claustrophobic. Ever since my brother Tom rolled me up tight on a Turkish rug. I couldn't move my arms. I felt helpless; try that once. Then Tom sat on me. To keep me quiet, Tom dropped a marble into my mouth every time I opened my mouth to cry out, but I outsmarted my brother Tom."

Clark's interest peaked. "How so? What did you do, Snarky?"

"I swallowed all ten of his marbles, that's what." Then I chuckled. "When he had no more marbles, he set me free. But I could never call your sweet wife Connie and sing a *Centerville fight song* for a prank or to pull on your chain, as you just said. Why would I?"

"Hold it right there. How did you know it was a *Centerville's fight song* he sang to her, Cameron? I never said that it was a *Centerville's fight song*."

"You really think it could be me making those telephone calls, Mr. Clark? Really, me?"

"You're damn right I do. On the margins, everyone is out to get me, you know, not just you?"

Ironically-as it might seem-we had our home telephone phone installed in the middle of June-for, my seventeenth birthday-but I felt that little fact, if known, might incriminate me more. So instead, I turned my attention away from Clark, hoping he would do the same to me. My eyes circled the rectangular locker room. Then they stopped. I read these stirring words written in bold yellow chalk on the portable chalkboard located directly behind Jim Clark:

Fasten your chin strap and keep it buckled,
You are about to enter the world,
Of Melville High School football,
Where young men reach their highest high,
And their lowest low, on Melville's noble field of football honor.

They really do take this game of football seriously at Melville, I thought.

"Captain Henri, didn't you say you knew this *band boy*? You were the first to recognize him when he entered a minute ago." Clark pointed to me.

"Yes. Well, I sort of know him, Coach."

"Sort of; what is the mystery here? Tell me what I don't already know, Captain Henri.

"Yes, well. I've seen him around campus, but we've never been formally introduced. I think we played a game of chess once."

"I won't ask you who won."

"Good. I think it was a Thursday. Yes, a Thursday. I know because it rained, and we were inside and not out on the playground."

"But you've seen him around the school campus, right?"

"Yes, I've seen him around school, Coach, in the school cafeteria at lunchtime, fourth period, sitting with the beautiful Angel White. You know, she won't talk to any of us football players."

"What, why is that? Is she the queen of the hop?"

"No, she thinks we're elitists and uncultured self-absorbed slobs who get catered to by the alumni, the fans, the teachers, and all the rest. The usual stereotype we football players have to overcome and endure daily, coached by a few, a select few who are jealous."

"She has no Melville football allegiance?"

"None?"

"No respect for our football program?"

"None."

"She thinks you boys and I are uncultured slobs who get catered to?"

"Yes."

"Well, we'll have to change her perception, Captain Henri. We have to win the hearts and minds of all our Melville students who think that way. We'll have to turn her before she turns us and all the others. Negative goodwill; I've seen it happen. If one disgruntled student speaks negatively about you or me, or our football program, it can take root and spread. This is how revolutions begin."

Clark stepped closer. So close, I caught the aroma of his chewing gum, *Spearmint*. Clark fired these rapid-fire questions. "Are you a Centerville spy? Have you ever been a Centerville spy? Are you loyal to Melville, or will you sell her for a few pieces of silver, Cameron? Are you a mercenary? Tell me the truth, now."

"Being a spy is not my forte. I love Melville, and I'm loyal to her. I'll stand beside her and guide her and defend her. I'll take no money. I'll accept no bribe. My loyalty cannot be bought. I'll make that pledge now. And if you allow me to stay and play, I will make you proud. But if the loyal Centerville supporters capture me, I'll remain quiet. I'll only give my captors and my interrogators my name, address, and our party line *phone number*."

"Wait, hold up. I thought you didn't have a telephone, Cameron?" An ominous murmur spread like an Asian Pacific Ocean tsunami across the Melville locker room. All eyes shifted toward me again with renewed interest.

"Did I say we didn't have a phone? I was speaking hypothetically. Well, now we have a phone, probably then, but not before."

"Are you playing me, *Snarky*? I'm not a moron, you know?"

"Do you really think he's a mole, Coach?" Captain Henri asked. "Is that what you are saying?"

"Well, there's definitely something wrong here, Henri. Money does strange things to entice young boys who have none. I've seen it happen. And then add a pretty teenage pubescent anti-Melville football girl to the mix, whose only loyalty is to her band and to her band friends, but not us. That can be explosive. If we let it go and do nothing, it can destroy a strong football program."

"If we can't trust the sweet and pretty Angel White, how can we trust Stevie Tyler Cameron in the world? Paul Henri asked Clark calmly.

Clark's eyes gleamed as if a light went on in his head. His eyes searched the locker room as if there were Centerville spy's everywhere, hidden in unfamiliar places. What crazy world had I entered? In the tipsy curvy world of Melville football, where paranoia runs rampant, concerns about the spies were taken seriously. It seemed bizarre, surreal, and unnatural. Had they ever caught a spy?

Clark continued his close-up and personal investigation and interrogation of me. "Where were you born, Cameron?"

"Melville, Sir."

"On what street?"

"Maple Street, Sir."

"You do know all nine of my veteran varsity football players sitting here?"

"Well, yes, sir, I know them all. But they don't know me."

"Well, that's strange, isn't it? Don't you find that strange, Cameron?"

"Well, yes, sir, I suppose it's strange."

"How do you do that, Son?"

"How do I do what, Sir?"

"How did you spend *eleven years* in the Melville public school system, and no one here knows your damn name?"

"I thought to *get that Band Boy* was my damn name." The veterans chuckled.

"But why don't they know you better?" Clark pointed at his nine seniors.

"Well, if you get your backside kicked every time you walk down the halls of Melville High School and get stuffed into lockers before every class, you soon learn not to walk down those halls. It can be a detriment to your health, like smoking. I've been stuffed into too many lockers, hit on and pounded on, and beaten until my arms, back, and shoulders were black and blue. So, I stay on the fringes, Sir. *I dart in, and I dart out.* Have you never been stuffed head first, upside down into a school locker, and left there until the end of the day? Try that!"

Clark's eyes narrowed. "Have you never been tortured for three days? Deprived of food and water and hung by your arms above your head until both your shoulders are pulled out of their sockets, and you pass out from the pain? *Try that!* Clark mumbled something indistinctly before he continued. "You said you stay on the fringes, hide in the shadows, and are seldom seen. Is that right, Cameron?"

"Yes, Sir, pretty much so, Mr. Clark." I felt concerned and deep sorrow for what else Clark endured and did not tell us about his time as a soldier spent on Bataan during World War 11.

"What, Coach? What are you thinking?"

"I was just wondering. So, tell me, Cameron. Who seated here is eating your lunch? Which one of my varsity football boys are you allowing to steal your lunch money?"

"Why do you ask me that personal question, Mr. Clark? I never said anyone ate my lunch or took my lunch money."

"Well, I would take your damn lunch money and make you carry my books as well. I might even have you polish my shoes, wash my car, and rake leaves. Once you let someone else compromise who you are, Cameron. You will be theirs until you stand tall, and… So, I ask you again. Who is your lunchroom offender? Is he seated here, Cameron? If so, point to him." Clark said.

"Don't hesitate, Cameron. You don't need a lawyer. We're not going to sue anybody. We don't need a lineup. Just answer the question. Is the *perp* seated here?" Captain Henri said.

I knew the word *perp* was short for perpetrator from the G-Men crime books I read in the Melville public library. I knew if I pointed to the offender, there would be hell to pay, and if I didn't point to the offender, it would further confirm to Clark I was a part of the problem. To deflect questions, I said. "Did you know I've never entered your football locker room until today? Not once. I always read those no admittance band boy signs and walked away and never had the nerve to enter and ask to try out for the team. But not today; your locker room is much smaller than I imagined, Mr. Clark."

"Quit lollygagging, Cameron, your stalling," Clark said.

Caught between two bad choices, I raised my right hand slowly and reluctantly. With no better option, I pointed to the one veteran varsity football player who represented the American heartland, Melville's soul and hope, and, some say, America. The glue that held this team and this football-crazed town on their shoulders, like Atlas, held the world every Friday night in the fall. He was Melville's undisputed football king, hero, lover boy, and four-year veteran and tight right end, *Romping Ronnie Dudiak*."

"*Romping* Ronnie Dudiak, huh?" Well, well, the Board of Education president's son. Who would have thought? Hmm, it's always the one you least suspect that surprises the most. We will deal with you later, Dudiak, but for the record, Cameron, I would never have given Dudiak up, never, never, never. I wouldn't have given Ronnie Dudiak up, or any bully, for that matter. I just wouldn't have."

"Despite the dire consequences, Mr. Clark?" I asked.

"Yes. You would have to torture me first, and then I would still resist. It's my code. It's called pride. Something a band boy wouldn't understand. But you apparently have no pride and no conviction or honor? Then when you gave him up, you pushed your part of the problem over to someone else, didn't you, Cameron? Those do-gooders who help you the most, I believe, are hurting you the most. It makes you dependent and them co-dependent. It sounds like a contradiction, does it not, Cameron?" Clark said.

"Yes, sir, it does."

"That makes you the victim. Everyone feels sorry for the victim, and you avoid taking any responsibility. Let me summarize."

Ronnie Dudiak ate your lunch?'

"Yes."

"And he took your lunch money too?"

"Yes."

"And you allowed it because he looked hungry?"

"Yes."

"And you probably felt sorry for him?"

"Yes, how did you know?"

"So you fed him your lunch, and you did without eating, and the payoff was you get to feel like a Good Samaritan, I suspect?"

"Yes, that's right, Mr. Clark."

Clark let out a deep sigh. "Now, doesn't that beat all I ever heard?

"So, you were the reason Ronnie Dudiak went off his weight reduction training table, huh?"

"Yes, I suppose so."

"Well, that explains a few things. But this is what I need to know now. Why did you give up your lunch and your lunch money to Ronnie Dudiak so easily without a fight? That's what I don't understand."

I felt the stress building inside me. Then I remembered my brother Tom's remedy for stress relief:

When stressed, Stevie relaxes, smiles broadly, and then breathes deeply three times because people who are stressed unconsciously hold their breath.

So, I smiled broadly, took three deep breaths, and felt much better.

"What would you have me do, Mr. Clark?" I asked.

"You could take yourself less seriously, Cameron? Why didn't you laugh it off or walk away? Or tell him no. Or tell him hell no and then back it up? Dudiak does not weigh much more than you do, *wet*. Maybe twenty or twenty-five pounds more or less? He is near your size, maybe three inches taller. Otherwise, he is just another kid on the block who puts his pants on the same way you do." Clark said easily, seemingly not understanding my good sense and logical reluctance to tangle with the four-year Melville varsity football star, *Romping Ronnie Dudiak*.

On page 41, the Melville student school policy states: In a case of being bullied, the person being bullied should first ask the bully to cease and desist. Suppose the bully does not cease and desist. In that case, the student must report the incident to a higher authority, like a teacher, school principal, or an adult. I had to give Jim Clark his due. It was true. I was part of the problem. Because I didn't stand on my own two feet and say no, or say hell no or follow the school policy and report the incident to a higher authority. Instead, I caved in and gave up my lunch and my lunch money. I remembered what Edmund Spencer wrote:

Throughout all past time, there has been a ceaseless devouring of the weak by the strong.

I then recalled what the American poet Robert Frost wrote:

Something we were withholding made us weak,

Until we found it was ourselves.

On October 29, 1941, Winston Churchill spoke about *never giving up* on the high school boys of the Harrow School in England, where Churchill once attended:

Never give in. Never give in. Never, never, never, never,

In nothing, great or small, large or petty,

Except for convictions of honor and good sense,

Never yield to force. Never yield to the apparently overwhelming Might of the enemy.

Clark knew he had won his point-handedly without the need for my rebuttal said. "Ok, let's move on before the underclassmen arrive. You said you know all nine of my varsity football players seated here, right?"

"Yes, sir, I know them all. But I know your team Doctors son, Lax Exley, is the best, Sir."

"Maybe Lax Exley will vouch for him, Coach." Captain Henri said. "That could clear him or smear him."

Clark turned to face my friend, Lax Exley. "*Lax Exley* put this puzzle together for us. I want the *truth*!"

CHAPTER FIVE
THE ROAD LESS TRAVELED

"Do you really want the *truth,* Coach?" "No, no, lie to me, *Exley*. Of course, I want the truth! This puzzle needs to be solved now! Tell me; is your friend, Cameron, a damn paid mercenary, an underground mole, was he sent here by Centerville's head football Coach, Gary Lee Thorn? Don't give me one of your long-winded walk-around-the-barn stories. Cut to it fast, Exley."

"But you will need to know who they are to better understand what they are. I'm probably the only Melville varsity football player who speaks *to* the band and not *at them*. I think I understand them and they me. We communicate. Granted, they are a peculiar bunch in some ways. But on the whole, our Melville band is credible. But seriously, no one gives a hoot about the band. They spend long hours practicing, just like we do in all kinds of weather. They provide half-time entertainment for our fans and our opponent's fans and give the team support. But no one gives them *respect* or shows them the appreciation they deserve because they are considered non-essential. After all, a football game can be played without them. So, I recommend-hence forth after every game-we as a sensitive, caring team-stroll over to the band section and thank our Melville marching band for all they do."

"Yeah, ok, fine, sure, we'll be more sensitive and show them a little more respect. But is Cameron a Centerville spy? That is the $64,000 question on the table now, Exley."

According to the T.V. Guide, the $64,000 question was the first big-money television quiz show. It ran for three years, from 1955-58.

"They call us varsity football players, *the swells,* you know, Coach," Lax said.

"So, we are *the swells, huh, Exley?* Is that what our Melville Band calls us behind our backs? Is that why you bully them?"

"Yes, Coach. Everyone knows that Melville football players are stuck up and conceited and get and expect adulation as a God-given right. But then the scene turns dark and sinister, Coach. Too much power corrupts. During school hours, we get away with murder. Teachers do give us a bye. We slam the band boys into lockers, give them wedgies, shove them into the girl's locker room, lock them inside our own lockers and make them late for your gym class so you will swat them with your gold engraved whistle. We degrade and belittle them constantly so we can have a good belly laugh at their expense like we feel they do to us.

"So why do you do that?

"Because it's easy, and we can."

"Because it's easy, and you can? This makes no sense."

"Everyone has a little sadism in them, Coach, I guess."

"Some day's hard to face the morning mirror," Clark said.

Lax sighed, showing some remorse.

"So, you are telling me you mostly pick on someone who is less able to defend themselves and can't or won't fight back?"

"Sure, that's pretty much it. *We get our kicks on route 66,* antagonizing band boys and not respecting the band girls too, sometimes." Lax said.

Route 66 ran from Chicago, Illinois, and went through Missouri to Los Angeles, California. The rhythm and Blues song *Route 66* Lax mentioned was first sung by Nat King Cole and composed in 1946 by Bobby Troup.

Clark turned and spoke to his nine seniors sternly. "So, you're the ones who bully the band boys and some band girls. Have I heard about you? You give our football program a bad name?" All eight of their heads dropped low. Paul Henri did not. He had never antagonized the band. But then again, he never stopped it. We provided too much fun and laughter. Then I remembered. I expected someone else to fight my battles and rescue me.

"What do you have to say for your sad selves?" Clark said to the *perps*.

Lax, who loved to talk, answered first. "The fact is, Coach, we're very quick-fisted, mean, and aggressive. Something you cherish, but they don't. We kick sand in all their faces over at Bob Howard's Lake Resort and steal their beach towels just to hear them squeal like pigs. We love to watch them run into the cold lake water just to make the older classy hoity-toity beach girls laugh."

"Is that why you do it? To make some airheads laugh?"

"Yes, but we're having fun at the band boy's expense. I know. I know it's not our finest hour."

"When you bully the Melville band-boys, what do they do? Do they ever fight back? Do they know you are just clowning around? Acting a fool?"

"No, no, they never fight back, Coach. That's what makes it so sweet. That's the beauty of it. Suppose they would stand up once and punch one of us in the nose-as hard as they could-we would stop. Nobody likes a hard punch in the nose."

"They just stand there and take it? That's it?" Clark asked.

"Yes, unfortunately."

"Do they cut and run?"

"No, Sir."

"Is that the truth, Cameron? You never cut and run. You stand your ground?"

"Well, yes sir, pretty much so, except my friend Lax Exley left out the worst part, the forcible removal of our swim suit then they hang them on the top of the resort flag pole up high where old glory flies. If you stay and stand your ground, Mr. Clark, this is what you get."

"Hmm, I see. I'm intrigued. So, what do you do then, Cameron?"

"Well, we ran as fast as we could into the lake where we treed water until dark. Then we ran out just as fast and quickly climbed to the top of the flag pole to get our swimsuits. But they rush in from hiding in the bushes and the brambles, grease the flag pole, and sometimes throw on some gasoline and then light it. Then they giggle and laugh when we band boys slide down that hot metal flag pole and burn our hands, thighs, and toques."

"Ok, we get the picture. Is that true, Exley?"

"Yes, well, sometimes we do act sophomoric and juvenile, Coach."

"Well, you won't get an argument on that from me, Exley."

"But coach, honestly, you never saw anything funnier than watching our band boys slide down that tall slippery flag pole and catch their bare bottoms on fire. Now that's funny." Lax said. All the football seniors laughed, and tears came to their eyes, remembering. Having more fun than anybody ought to have.

"*Laxly*, your idea of fun is downsizing someone else. Someday that dog will bite you."

"Yes, well, the first Coach, must I remind you again, my name is not *Laxly*. It's *Lax Exley*. I've played varsity football for you for three years, and sometimes you mistakenly call me La*x*ly. And that's *not ok*, Coach. I deserve more respect."

Clark interrupted my thoughts. "Do you see what just happened here, Cameron? Did you see how ax Exley stood up for himself? He has pride in himself and would not be trampled on like someones damn dirty floor mat. Lax Exley, you just regained my respect, son. Do you see what he did, Cameron?"

"Yes, Sir, I can see clearly, Mr. Clark." I found it ironic that my friend Lax was a major player and demanded respect when he gave none in the band none. There I go again. Expecting someone else to give me what I did not earn.

Clark's eyes narrowed once again. "Ok, I'm beginning to smell a *rat,* Captain Henri. I think we've found our *motive.* I think we found our mole."

"So, you think Cameron's a mole, a Centerville plant, looking for revenge on our football player's chicanery, monkeyshines, and tomfoolery? Captain Henri said, his face very serious.

"Yes, but the question still remains, Captain Henri. Is he a mercenary or not? We now know he has a strong motive, *revenge.* But does he harbor any *malice?"*

"Well, it's possible, Coach." Captain Henri said. "But what if he harbors only a little *malice* due to his harsh treatment by the senior football players? They do get unruly at times. I've seen it. But that doesn't make him a paid Centerville spy? Does it?"

"Yes, well, that's the key point. That's what we would need to prove beyond a shadow of a doubt. Is there malice? Without provable *malice,* we have no case. We must acquit." Clark said unapologetically.

"Maybe we're overthinking this whole thing, Coach. Maybe a spy would not be so obvious, would he? Sit down and think about it. First, he showed up here today, late. Not a good thing. Then he came in here wearing naval sunglasses, a blue Superman T-shirt, Bermuda shorts, a white belt, white socks tennis shoes. That draws a lot of attention, you know." Captain Henri said. "We are a blue jean and plaid shirt town."

Clark looked at me hard once again from head to toe. "He's certainly not a slave to fashion, Captain Henri, dressed like a gigolo." Everyone laughed, of course, at Clark's cheap humor, except Clark.

"Is he a Christian? Does he go to church regularly? That's what we need to know, Captain Henri. Does he believe in an almighty God?"

"Coach Clark, why are you asking Cameron if he is a Christian, believes in God, or goes to church regularly?

"Because I believe *a true Christian* who believes in God, Captain Henri, would find it difficult to tell us a *lie*."

"But that's a personal question. We don't ask that here in Melville. We don't discuss religion or politics." Captain Paul Henri reminded Clark.

"Yes, I'm a Christian. I go to church often. I believe there was a man named Noah, there was an ark and a flood, and I believe in, *thy kingdom comes, thy will be done, on earth, as it is in heaven.*

The Universe didn't just happen, you know. Something had to *create it*. Maybe the cosmos came from a black hole or nothing, right? It's like, which came first, the chicken or the egg? Has that ever been solved? The key question to be answered is done. I believed in Jesus, and was he the son of God, and did he rise from the dead?"

"If God is all-powerful, why would he need billions of years to make the earth evolve and all its living things? I'm curious. Why not do it in a day." Clark asked me.

"I see no conflict, Mr. Clark. God took six days, using *his time* to make everything. It's like he planted a garden here on earth and then watched it grow. I think what confuses everybody is the total lack of scientific knowledge about who we are and where we came from. The Bible explains all of that. Science is still searching. *Let there be light, and there was light.* Remember that? But I have a problem with the church, Mr. Clark." I said.

Clark's eyes rose. "What kind of problem, Cameron?"

"Sir?"

"What kind of problem do you have, he asked?"

"Oh, I have a sitting problem."

"You have a sitting problem?"

"Yes, sir, I can't sit still for very long."

"What happens?"

"I get the heebie-jeebies."

Clark smiled. "Well, you sure do think, talk and walk strangely, Cameron. The stranger than all of these boys seated here combined. Surely you must know that?"

"Yes, sir. I get that all the time." Like Henri David Thoreau wrote in his book *Walden Pond*:

If a man loses pace with his companions, perhaps it is because he hears a different drummer. Let him step to the music he hears, however, measured or far away.

"tell me, Cameron. Did we do something to make you *angry*? Something I don't know about? Something I did or said? Are you here to punish me?"

"Angry, punish you. No, sir, I put no thought into that. Why do you ask."

"When you came to the *fork in the road* on Algona and Gibbons, why did you choose to walk up Algona on a hot sunny summer day like this one?"

When I came to that fork in the road, it was like Yogi Berra said:

When you come to a fork in the road, take it.

"So, you took it."

"Yes, sir, but that road sure is dusty?"

"It might be dusty, Cameron, but it won't be dull. I'll promise you that."

In late August, to save the town money and keep the dust down, Melville's Street department sprayed the dusty unpaved roads with oil. They called it Texas Tea.

"So why did you really take our fork in the road when the left fork is much more scenic and beautiful and paved for the school buses, you know."

I remembered what the American poet Robert Frost wrote about coming to a fork in the road:

When you come to a fork in the road,
Sometimes it is better to take the one less traveled,
And that will make all the difference.

"I chose *the road less traveled*, Mr. Clark."

"You say you chose *the road less traveled*. Surely there are many other things you could be doing, like swimming at Bo Howard's Beach on a hot day like today, well maybe not at Bo Howards Beach, which could get even hotter. Why have you chosen Melville football? Why us? Clark asked. He wouldn't let up.

"I come with a good soul and high intentions like Lancelot did to Camelot, Sir, to fulfill my mission."

"Did you really come here today with a good soul and high intentions, or did you come here to cause mayhem and destroy my *Camelot*?"

CHAPTER SIX
CAMELOT

"Funny you should ask. On our spring trip, our Melville marching all one hundred and ten rode in two Grey Hound buses to New York City to see that very Broadway Musical. Have you also seen Camelot, the musical, Sir?" "Yes, of course, I've seen Camelot, the musical. *I'm married*, Cameron. And if I recall, Sir Lancelot destroyed Camelot, betrayed King Arthur, and he started a very nasty war. Many valiant Knights of the Round Table were senselessly killed. That shows you what trouble young romantic love can do."

"Do you think Lancelot purposely caused all that trouble, Sir?"

"Well, the facts are the facts. Facts can be stubborn things. King Arthur was my hero, Cameron. But Sir Lancelot smashed Camelot and King Arthur's altruistic vision into a thousand pieces for what, a few moments of heated pleasure?"

"But sir, Lancelot and Guinevere were deeply in love."

"Romantic love is overestimated, overstated, and wasted on the young. That's why I forbid every Melville football player to date or mate during the football season. You boys will thank me later."

I heard a few groans from the vets.

"But Lancelot had *good intentions*, Mr. Clark. *His heart was pure as fresh white snow."*

"Who talks like this, Henri? Remind me?" Clark said.

Henri shook his head sideways then his blue eyes lit. "Russell Mc Mackey, class of 58, Coach.*"*

"The Thespian!"

"Yes."

"Wacky Mc Mackey?"

"Yes. I believe you called him that, Sir." Do you remember him, Coach?"

"Yes, I sure do. He sure was a pistol. Where is he now, Henri, in jail?"

"No, Beijing, China, I think. Last I heard."

"China, huh? Is he growing a *cue?*"

"No, I don't think so, Coach. That went out of style about 40 years ago over there."

The Chinese wore a *cue* as a sign of *loyalty to their emperor.* It resembled what we call a braided ponytail. The emperor killed everyone who didn't wear a cue. It showed they were not loyal to him.

"Did you know Russell Mc Mackey finished college?" Henri said.

"He has a college degree. What in?"

"English."

"You need an English degree to teach English in China?"

"Apparently so, Coach."

"Hmm."

All I wanted was to be allowed to try out for his football team. But Clark's penetrating voice and probing questions made me nervous. My thoughts were occupied with vague concepts about the team and Clark. I had no idea how things were going to turn out for me, which made me even a little more strung out. So, I tried to be light and airy, thinking a shallow answer as to who I was and why I was here would suffice.

"They say you have a tough football training program here, Mr. Clark. So, I figured, hey, maybe I should try out for your team, get in shape, tighten up a few weak muscles, build a little hard muscle here and there, and gain a little weight. I mean, hey, what have I got to lose?

"Your two front teeth!" Captain Paul Henri replied. Everyone laughed, Clark included.

"Ok, enough jaw-boning and being cutesy, Cameron, let's cut to the chase. Quit stringing us along. No more platitudes. You're not here for a challenging physical endurance training program, are you?" Clark asked.

"Coach is right, Cameron. That dog doesn't hunt!" Henri said. "Give us something to hang onto. Throw us a rope or a lifeline. A mole can lie dormant for many years until activated."

Clark turned quickly toward me. "Can we trust you to be *loyal* to Melville? Or will you sell her for a few pieces of silver? Why are you really here? Is it for personal glory, fame, to impress a girlfriend, or to spy for revenge, or to make some money?"

"What do you want from me, Coach, an oath of loyalty?"

"Why attach yourself to this difficult endeavor, Cameron? Truthfully, quit dancing around us. What is the real skinny, the deeper truth? There has got to be something more here. I sense it. I asked you whether you are a mole. And you said no. I asked you whether you are a damn Centerville plant. And you said no. Only a damn fool would try out for our varsity athletic team with no real reason, purpose, or no known motivation. Everyone here has a core reason for being here. But from the looks of it, I don't think you do have one. However, if we dig deep enough, we will find yours, Cameron."

I feared his line of questioning. I believe one's deeper motivations are the best-kept secret. I believe they tend to lose their strength, conviction, and power once voiced and laid bare for all to hear. They shrivel up, die and then disappear like in a puff of white magician's smoke. Captain Paul Henri and the veterans studied me hard as if I was some space alien that came from Mars or the dark side of the moon. I felt a little uncomfortable, yet I didn't leave my place. I was determined.

"Look, I live in Melville. I go to school and church in Melville, and both my father and my brother played football for you here at Melville. My grandmother has always lived and worked in Melville down at Mr. Saperstein's bakery. Therefore, I believe I have some *persuasive legitimacy* here, Mr. Clark. Isn't that enough?"

"I don't get it. Why Melville football? Why not try out for the cross country, the school's Chess Team? Henri says you play well, Tidily Winks. Anything other than football? Why choose us? Why chase our crazy horizon?"

I felt worn down. I had no more glib answers. No more ballrooms to dance into. The cakewalk music stopped, and I had no empty chair to sit in. But I felt I had one last chance to convince Jim Clark of my loyalty. So, I gathered my courage and told the truth.

"I quit the Melville marching band as a senior to try out for Melville football at my deceased war hero father's last dying request. And so, I stated my mission."

But why my football program Cameron? Why my football team?"

"Our deceased war hero father, John 'the Scott' Cameron, had incredible respect for you and your character-building football training program. He felt your tough demanding program would serve us well in life and, God forbid, also in war, as it served him well in the Second World War. Our father, who is now in heaven, believed playing Melville football would make us *stronger*, *improve our character, develop our leadership skills,* and *better prepare us for life* in his absence. He felt there was something intangible playing *football* here at Melville could teach us. Is that true, Coach? Will playing football at Melville make me stronger and better prepare me for life without my mother and father?"

"I don't know whether playing Melville football makes you a better person or builds one's character. I can't say whether or not playing Melville football will prepare you for life without a father's support or a mother's love. But what I do know is this. If you make this team and finish the season and you have courage, they won't kick sand in your face and hang your bathing suit up on the flag pole at Bo Howard's Beach and Lake Resort anymore. I can promise you that, Cameron."

Something stirred inside me. The thought of my never being embarrassed ever again in front of Angel White and everyone else at school or at Bo Howard's Beach Resort seemed highly desirable. The very thought of growing stronger seemed appealing also.

Helen Hays once said:

Every human being on this earth is born with a tragedy,
And it isn't original sin,
He's born with the tragedy
That he has to grow up.
A lot of people don't have the courage to do it.

Whether I had that courage, I did not know. There is little doubt of my need to grow up. "Now, may I ask you a personal question, Mr. Clark?"

"Yeah, sure, shoot Cameron, take your time but make it quick the underclassmen are coming any minute now, and chaos will ensue. It always does."

"Melville football, what is in it for you? What is your payoff? "What is your motivation, Mr. Clark? Are you happy here at Melville?" All nine of Jim Clark's veteran varsity football players listened hard to my bold questions for Mr. Jim Clark.

Clark pointed at me nervously. "You're good. You're really good, Cameron! What is my motivation? Why do I coach football here at Melville, you ask? What is my payoff? Am I happy here? I ask myself these same questions daily, and so does my beautiful Bo Howard Beach beauty pageant-winning trophy wife, Connie. God knows teaching is certainly not for the money. But I can now happily conclude, after much consideration, I'm so happy here at Melville High School that I could just *jump and fart*." Everyone snickered. "Excuse my sailor language. I know that sometimes I'm told I can be a bit *crass*. But that's my charm, and this is a football locker room, not a church pew or a confessional. They say a football locker room is the closest thing to an army barracks. Cameron, what do you think about that?"

"Well, I've never been in an army barracks, sir, so I cannot compare, Mr. Clark."

"Look, Cameron, there are thousands of jobs out there that pay more money and require less time and certainly cause me less stress but have less vacation time. This job is my best fit. In teaching, we get the summers off. Summertime is my time. I can bass fish, play gin rummy, barbecue, play golf, swim, read a good book, take a good nap in my hammock, and travel as far as my meager base teacher's salary and my old woody will carry me. Look, I get paid seven hundred and fifty-two dollars for coaching varsity football before taxes. The board of education throws me a mere two hundred dollars more for watering and taking care of the football field during the summer."

"That is not much money, Coach," Henri said. "The Saint Louis Budweiser Brewery pays more than that to drive a beer truck."

"Yes, but look at the perks, Captain Henri. Instead of long-haul driving and being away from home. I get to stand in front of a crowd of fickle Melville fans every Friday night, for three glorious fall months, in an attempt to bring this community together and to cause our team members to bond. Then the Saturday morning paper arrives, The Melville Times, is delivered to my door or somewhere close. I step out, pick it up, open it to the sports page and start reading *Bret's Corner*. And what do I see? Bret Hart rips me apart like a crazed wild dog on steroids. If Bret Hart's brains were dynamite, Captain Henri wouldn't have enough powder to blow his nose with. Now that's the darn truth."

"Then why do this gig, Coach?" I asked.

"This is my way of giving back. I try to give the boys of Melville something special, a good experience like I had. Something they will carry with them for the rest of their lives. I want you lads to be mentally and physically prepared for the ten league games we play this season and for your military service if ever you are called to duty by the draft. I fear this generation may not hold on to what freedom it is given. I don't ever want to see any American boy ever go off to war to fight for my freedom without the proper fighting equipment. They sent us off to war with hand grenades that never worked and artillery shells that were duds. They had cut back on the military funding for our country's preparedness believing World War I was *the war to end all wars."*

Everything I knew about Clark I read in the Melville Times newspaper. Mostly in Bret Hart's sports column or his radio sports talk show. Bret said that before the war, Jim Clark, fresh out of Missouri University, got married to Connie Jean Bishop, a Melville graduate. Upon his return from the big war, he coached football and track and taught Drivers Education and Physical Education. He joined the local teacher's union to hopefully boost his pay and maintain job security. He contributed to the Missouri State Retirement System, counting the years until his retirement.

Everyone knew he was a prisoner of war in the Philippines. They looked for cracks in his mental and emotional state. They wondered if he was fit to be a head football coach and a high school physical education teacher or if he would at any moment crack. I couldn't picture that. Not Jim Clark. I felt his brutal experiences only made him stronger. He had turned out to be one of the bests. But Victor D. Huron Melville's High School principal and the Board of Education often said they held their collective breath. But I wondered, like everyone else, how much the Pacific war, the horrific Bataan Death March, and his near-death prisoner-of-war experiences affected Jim Clark mentally and emotionally and how he coached this team.

The Melville Board of Education president, Carl Dudiak, is known to have said Clark's reason for staying one more year is his desire, not his *obsession* with going *undefeated* and achieving *two hundred career wins.* Something Clark would neither confirm nor deny.

In his sports column, Bret Hart often quoted Clark's nemesis Gary Lee Thorn who predicted this could be Jim Clark's final year of teaching Physical Education and coaching football and track at Melville High School. He did not say why. Centerville's Coach Gary Lee Thorn also said Melville's football team *would not* go undefeated this year and would not win the all-important last game with Melville's arch-rival Centerville, and therefore, Coach Jim

Clark *would not* go undefeated or get his coveted two hundred career wins. Thorn said he would personally see to that.

"Do you play the *bugle*, Cameron?" Clark asked, making a sharp pivot away from himself.

"No, sir."

"Well, huh, why not?"

"I don't have access."

"If you had access, could you play *reveille or charge on the bugle*?"

"Yes. They are all standard bugle calls. Why do you ask?"

"Can you play Taps, also?"

"Yes, of course. It's not too tricky once you get the first note."

"Tell me, how many other Melville band instruments can you play?"

"Nine, I play the tuba, piccolo, flute, clarinet, trumpet, drum, Sax, French horn, and piano. Everything musical is based on the piano, you know."

"No, I didn't know. Why the drum?"

"Without the drum, we would have no rhythm, you see."

Just then, Billy Strivectin, Melville's drum major, walked into the Melville football locker room, breathing heavily. He wore a Superman T-Shirt like mine and naval pilot sunglasses like mine. He sheepishly walked over to me and stood in front of me, giving me a weird yet beamish gaze. I greeted Billy with a handshake and remained standing beside him to give him support.

"What's your name?" Clark asked Billy sharply.

"Billy Strivectin, Coach, coming to you directly from the Melville band reporting for your morning briefing for *senior footballers*. Is this it?"

Clark sighed. "Not another squirrely, no nothing, ill-advised, toilsome, band-playing band boy, Captain Henri?"

"It looks like it, Coach. We now have two *band boys* who I'll bet don't know their watch pocket from an empty Dixie Ice-Cream cup."

"And if all this is not bad enough, Henri, too, has the unmitigated gall to arrive at our first-morning brief for seniors *late w*hen everyone else made the necessary painstaking arrangements to arrive here on time. Am I right, Captain Henri, or am I right?"

"When you're right, you're right, Coach," Henri said. "Facts are difficult to refute."

"And now Henri, I suppose we *four coaches* and correct me if I'm wrong, are expected to take these two rough cut gems-who came from who knows what outhouse, garbage bin, or excrement of the bowels of the earth-wash them off real clean, and polish them up real shiny and in less than thirty days, have them ready to play against a first-class varsity football team-our cross-town arch-rival-

La Santos! By damn, I don't think it can be done, Captain Henri, do you?"

"No, Coach, that's not much time to train and teach two inexperienced senior *band boy's* all the rudiments of hard-nosed Melville football in less than three weeks and have them ready to play against a seasoned, hard-hitting team like La Santos in our season opener."

Clark's mind drifted. "What have I done to deserve these two band boys on the same day, Captain Henri?" Clark walked closer to Billy Strivectin and me. "Tell me, what position might you wish to try out for, Strivectin?"

"Why quarterback, of course!"

"Why *quarterback*, of course, of course, quarterback, of course!" Clark said. "Over one hundred boys will be trying out for eleven offensive and eleven defensive positions today, Billy. Some will try out at quarterback. They always do. But what would make me think that you would not choose a quarterback? It's flashy. You get to call the plays and throw some passes, a drum major's dream. But what makes you think you can handle being our *team leader*, Strivectin?"

"As drum major, I lead one hundred and ten band members through their precision drills, sir, and we have many formations. I personally choreographed almost all of them. I'm under extreme pressure to perform well with a ton of responsibility. If it goes well, I get the credit. If it goes sour, I get the blame, Sir. I'm also an Eagle Scout just like your big..."

Clark interrupted Billy. "Wait, what position did your father ask you to try out for, Cameron?"

"My father was very specific on that point, Mr. Clark. He wanted Tom and then me to play quarterback, of course, like he did, win the Golden Helmet and become *a Melville Man*. But that is what puzzles me the most, Coach. What exactly is a Melville Man, and why in the world would our father ever want my brother Tom and me to become one?"

Clark's eyes lit up like Melville's Fourth of July fireworks at Melville's Constitution Park.

"Captain Henri, will you please stand and tell these two football *rookies*, this unsullied knight of the round table and the drum major from hell, what *a Melville Man is*. And please speak to them from your heart, son."

"Sure, Coach, sure, gladly."

CHAPTER SEVEN
A MELVILLE MAN

Captain Paul Henri stood proudly as if reciting a favorite poem in Miss Roberta Stone's senior English class. He cleared his throat. He held his large hands at his side and held his square shoulders back. His chiseled chin was thrust forward. His head held up. His deep, raspy, base voice bounced off the freshly painted blue Melville locker room walls like a rubber ball. A Melville Man is:

A special man, quite unique these days. He's a stand-up guy: a leader of men, a team player, and highly respected. He believes in fair play and sportsmanship. He will be humble in loss as well as victory. He'll give his all and never give up on the field of honor until his last breath. He will fight through pain and fear till the very end. He'll leave nothing on the field of honor but his blood and his guts. He would knowingly die for his football brothers, knowing they would die for him. That, Coach Clark, is a Melville Man."

"When you have all eleven Melville men on the playing field willing to die for his football brothers, you will be hard to beat," Clark added.

I knew instantly I would never live up to Henri's depiction of a Melville man. No one could. I looked over at each of the veterans and studied them carefully. They were young, enthusiastic, and gong ho. I wondered why they were here. What motivation did they bare? "Coach, may I ask you a serious question?" Billy Strivectin asked Clark.

"Sure, Billy. We take questions seriously here, but not everyone likes the answers we provide. But you intrigue me, Strivectin, so fire away?"

"Do you issue a manual or study sheet so that I could study this Melville Man Philosophy more carefully?"

I heard chuckles and small laughter. "No, we don't issue manuals or study sheets here, do we, Henri?"

"No, it's either sink or swim here, Coach."

"But I can't swim." Billy acted concerned.

Captain Henri replied coldly. "Then you'll drown."

"That seems rather barbaric, does it not." Billy said, looking very distraught now."

"Yes, I guess maybe it does," Clark said. 'Does all this self-reliant macho Texas talk scare and confuse you, Billy?"

"Yes, it's true, Mr. Clark; your macho football world scares the hell out of me and most young boys I know. Can't you apply your strict, demanding mindset to this high school football squad? It's silly being so *gung-ho*. Have you never been mellow?"

"If you go out on the sacred field of battle and have ten Melville players and one individual whose mellow you don't have a team, Billy," Clark said. Melville football is part of the fabric of life in this small prairie town. You can't escape it. Everyone in Melville knows that come Friday night in the fall, Melville football is king. There is nothing like a good ole rough-and-tumble high school football game to bring out the community and pull the town together, rooting for the home team. Our football program builds tradition and social interaction and, of course, provides entertainment. It gives meaning to an otherwise boring Friday night in the fall of the year. I always take a minute to step out of the locker room to watch the band, the fans, the students, and their families arrive. They wear our red school colors proudly, and they leave happy when we win and sad and angry as a nest of disturbed hornets when we lose.

"You don't need to tell me how Melville football is part of this town's fabric of life," Billy said. "Our Melville marching band plays center stage at halftime. Our band, majorettes, our drill teams, color guard, flag squads, and cheerleaders are all caught in their power like a witch's spell. In the band, we are given music sheets to study and fun instruments to play. Once we learn how to read the music sheets and play our instruments, then we can enjoy playing our music forever. Does your team concept carry over for a lifetime, Coach?" Billy asked Clark.

"Well, we like to think it does. That might make a good doctoral thesis for someone here to write someday or a good sportsbook to prove my position."

"Our band leader, Milo Clem, says the music we play once learned well carries over for a lifetime and sounds beautiful like a raindrop falling in heaven. He says you love the song *Stardust*." Billy added.

"Yes, I love it, I really do, and so does my wife, Connie. She especially loves the first verse:"

And now the purple dusk of twilight time
Steals across the meadows of my heart.

"Someone calls the house and sings that verse. Do you know anything about that, Billy?"

Billy turned. "No, but I've heard you have collected the entire *Stardust collection*, composed by Hoagy Carmichael and the lyrics written by Mitchell Parish, Coach. I'm a collector too. You know, Coach."

"Billy can play 24 versions of Stardust," I said.

"But I keep trying to learn to play the other two," Billy replied.

Clark turned to face Captain Henri. "Do you remember that laundry basket caper?"

"Yes, sir. Sure do, sure, Coach. Who could forget that? Gary Thorn paid those two little people fifty dollars each to hide in our locker room laundry baskets to spy on us."

"Can you remember their darn names, Henri?"

"Sure, Coach, Mary, and Cary Pippins."

"Poppins, like Mary Poppins?"

"No, Coach, Pippins like Mary Pippins."

"Well, where do those Pippins live in a shoe?"

"No, Coach, they lived in our laundry baskets for two full weeks during spring training, hearing everything you said and watching everything you did."

All eyes moved to the two white canvas laundry baskets that sat near Coach Clark's office door.

"Where do they live?"

"I heard they lived downtown on Pershing Street."

"Do they still live there, now, Henri?"

"No, Coach, rumor has it that they moved to Centerville. They are now Coach Gary Lee Thorn's two most trusted and decorated football managers. It was an in-your-face promotion for being loyal spies, I suppose."

"He wouldn't stoop so low!"

"Apparently, he would, Coach, and he did. Instead of punishing someone for spying and doing wrong, he promotes them and then shuffles them around, like..."

"Like the deck chairs on the Titanic?"

"Yes. I know you hate that comparison, Coach."

"Yes, because good people lost their lives because of... Oh, never mind. Only God knows what secrets those two little people learned before being found out. Thorn will do anything to gain an advantage. I know Centerville's board of education quietly enacted a policy of *red-shirting* all of their eighth-grade football players to give them another year of maturity and practice while maintaining four years of varsity eligibility."

"They practice but do not play?" I asked.

"Yes, that's right."

"That gives Centerville quite an advantage over every other team they play and all the other teams in the Melville Valley Athletic League who do not *red-shirt*, you know," I said.

I raised my right hand.

"Then why won't the Melville Valley Athletic League coaches get together and vote to ban this unfair practice, Coach?"

"There is nothing the league can do if the parents and board of education sign off on it, like most of them do at Centerville, La Santos, and North Chamberlin, Cameron. We could do it, but I won't. We are better than that. If you want to know who we are, know this. Here at Melville, we practice sportsmanship and sports etiquette, and we promote the virtues of team spirit. That is who we are. We do not spy or take film of our opponent's play. We must foil every one of Thorn's attempts to spy. He only needs to succeed once, you know?"

"What else can we do to stop him?" Henri asked. "What must we do?"

"First, we must beef up security until this is no longer a target-rich environment. Second, we will seal off all the stadium entrance points for every practice and go into lockdown by posting guards at every gate. From now on, they must enter through the main stadium gate only. Third, tell Houdini, our head school custodian, to close all the school shades on the practice side of the school building once school starts. Our students and teachers don't need to see what we are doing on the practice field. And Henri…?"

"Yes, Coach."

"Remind me not to call Houdini *a janitor anymore*. I did once, and he almost tore my face off with a claw hammer. He has such a delicate, sensitive prideful soul. He now calls himself a *sanitary engineer,* and so must I. Houdini is the cog that makes this plant work. I respect any man who gets up early in the morning in the dark cold of winter and comes to work in all kinds of weather to fire up the coal furnace and tend the boilers to keep this place nice and warm and cozy for when the teachers and students arrive three hours later. I respect that. Henri, from now on, we must place a quota on the number of fans and loyal club members who come to watch us practice and keep a watch list."

"Keep a watch list, Coach?"

"Yes."

"Is that all, Sir?"

"No Henri, tell, Jay Houdini."

"Our sanitary engineer!"

"Yes, that's right. Tell Jay Houdini not to let anybody not on that watch list through that main gate. Did I say seal off *all* the other entrance points?"

"Yes, Coach."

"Good, because, Henri."

"Yeah, Coach."

"I don't know who I can *trust* anymore!"

"But don't you think you are being a little *paranoid,* Coach?" Henri asked.

"Well, I wouldn't be so damn *paranoid,* Henri, if they weren't all out to get me! During our games, emotions run high. Why, more than once, I've had to run off the field escorted by the town or State police to avoid a fight with our own fans, not theirs?"

"Our own Melville fans try to pick a fight with you, Coach, not the competitor's fans?" I asked Clark.

"If you did a case study of the typical Melville fan and you drilled deep below the surface, you would be surprised how crazy they really are, Cameron, but don't tell them I said so, or I will call you a darn liar. Bret Hart doesn't corner the market on *crazy,* you know. I can be crazy too."

'Do you know what makes this laundry basket caper so terrible? Captain Henri said coldly.

"No, what?" Clark said.

"They slept here right under our noses-now that's damn embarrassing-in our own laundry baskets, and we didn't even know it."

"They were sleeper cells," I said. I heard a few scattered laughs.

"Yes, and we may never know the extent of the damages his two spies may have inflicted on our football program," Clark said.

I raised my hand. "But don't you have someone who checks on things down here in your locker room, Coach, besides the janitor, I mean sanitary engineer?"

"Well, yes, we have Mike Carson, our football manager. But why do you ask, Cameron?"

"Well, why didn't Mike Carson stop this *laundry basket caper* in its tracks?"

"That's a good question, Cameron. The reason is Mike Carson always arrives late, just like you and Strivectin did today. Show me a man who reports late for an important meeting, and I will show you a self-centered, self-absorbed son of a witch. Do you know why people arrive late, Cameron?

"Because they think *their time* is more important than *yours*, sir?"

"Bingo, your right! You're right! That's it. They think their time is more important than ours, just like you two band boys did today.

You think you can come waltzing in here, any time you please? You think we are supposed to cater to you. Its self-importance that has gone a-muck. You need to plan better, start earlier and always allow extra time in case of an emergency. I cannot stress the importance of Punctuality!" Clark said.

I felt Clark wanted something more from Billy and me, something intangible. What that something was, I didn't know. Unsure of our true heading or course, we were about to enter uncharted waters. Obviously, there wasn't going to be an easy camaraderie between us. That much was certain.

Billy Strivectin eased closer and whispered this in my right ear.

"Cam, check your wristwatch."

I glanced down to check my wristwatch. Yep! Mickey's big hand was on the twelve; his little hand was on the eight. That's eight o'clock anywhere in the world. Now I felt totally vindicated. I *arrived on time!* Jim Clark had obviously started his briefing *early,* so I did not know. But what should I do? Should I speak up? I raised my hand.

"What is it now, Cameron?"

"Neither Billy nor I reported *late* for your morning briefing for seniors, sir."

"What? What! I beg your pardon?"

"Either your watch is wrong, or you simply began your morning brief early. That can happen, you know."

"Yes, that could happen, I suppose, like Frank Christian and Fatso Hurst switching their allegiance to Centerville. That could happen! Or like us defeating Centerville by thirty points this year. That could happen too. But don't bet your last dime or bottom dollar on it, Snarky."

"Maybe your watch is broken or needs cleaning. Have you considered that? My Mickey Mouse watch stops all the time if I don't rewind it- so I just shake it. It starts most of the time."

Clark stood closer.

"So you think my very expensive Gold Anniversary wristwatch is broken? This watch was an anniversary gift from my lovely wife, and it is, therefore, what I prize most above all things. It tells the perfect time all the time and always has. You see, it never needs rewinding. It tells me you and what's his name arrived here *late* today. Cameron, are you listening? Are we talking to ourselves here? Are you daydreaming? I said there was good news and bad news. The bad news is your Mickey Mouse wristwatch may be broken, Cameron. The good news is it is always right *twice a day*."

The veterans laughed. I noticed how Clark played to them. I found this to be offsetting. "With no disrespect for your intended, Coach, or to you, Captain Henri, but I believe your grand assessment of us *band boys* and our proposed degree of tardiness does not rise to a high level of possibility or authenticity."

"What?"

"I think he just said...."

"Yes, I know what he just said, Henri. I have great respect for anyone who states the truth, you know. And yes, I do have a tendency to embellish sometimes. But I have never in my recent memory been called a *liar* in such an agreeable fashion or manner."

Let's try this again. Did you two *band boy's* not read Bret Hart's article in the Melville Times stating the starting time for our senior briefing today? Maybe you didn't read Bret's article, is that it? That is it, isn't it, Strivectin, Cameron? You didn't read it*?"*

"No sir, we read it, Coach." We said in unison.

"Then tell me, what time did Bret Hart's article say we would begin our first-morning briefing for seniors?"

"8: A.M., sir?"

Billy's voice rose as if it were a question.

"No, no, no, Strivectin, that is *regular time, not Lombardi time."*

Billy raised his right hand.

"What is Lombardo time, Coach?"

For many years my brother Tom had a large poster of Vince Lombardi plastered on his bedroom door and a picture of his star quarterback, # 15, Bart Starr. Billy apparently thought Clark said *Lombardo time,* which was either the name of a famous Canadian-American *orchestra leader* named *Guy Lombardo* or that *red*

Italian table wine, Lombroso. I knew, of course, very well who Lombardi was. But I, too, had never heard of *Lombardi Time*.

"Captain Henri?"

"Yes, Coach?"

"I'm losing my patience here. Help me out. Sometimes the stupidity of a Melville band boy is *simply amazing*.

"Or *amazingly simple*." Captain Henri said.

"I think that is why I hate them so. Captain Henri, will you please stand and tell these two uninformed band *boy's* who *Vince Lombardi is.*"

"Sure, Coach, gladly."

Captain Paul Henri stood proudly as if reciting a poem. He held his large hands to his sides, held his square shoulders back; his chiseled chin thrust forward, and his voice, a raspy deep base.

"*Vince Lombardi* is the coach of the great Green Bay Packers Coach."

"And what time *is Lombardi time?*"

Lombardi time is fifteen minutes before the actual time stated."

"And why do we use *Lombardi time* here at Melville, Captain Henri?"

"Being prompt and punctual and arriving fifteen minutes earlier than the stated time for every team meeting and practice assures us that we'll never arrive late and always be on time. It makes a statement that says we're reliable, responsible, and trustworthy, the trademark of a *Melville man*."

"And, therefore?"

"And, therefore, these two band boy's reported *late* for your first-morning briefing for seniors, using *Lombardi time,* of course."

I remembered what Marilyn Monroe said about *being on time*:

I've been on a calendar, but I've never been on time.

Apparently, Marilyn Monroe never considered being on time as important as Jim Clark.

Clark removed his red baseball cap from his head with his left hand and scratched his head. His eyes narrowed like Clint Eastwood's again.

"I've just begun to have a stronger distaste for *you* and all those no-name, tuba-touting, music-shouting, half-crazed Milo Clem hero-worshiping Melville band boy's, who come waltzing in here every year, full of hope and prayer with high apple pie in the sky hopes and prom glitter in their eyes and no credible football playing experience. Yet, you want me to allow you to try out for this man's football team as a senior just to say you made the team, play a few quarters to get a Melville football letter, and wear to all the sock hops to impress the Melville girls. Does that resemble you, Billy Strivectin, and you, Cameron?"

We were both stunned and remained as quiet as church mousses. We didn't have a credible reply. So we chose silence.

"Take a seat, *boys*, but stick around. Your Real-Ville education is about to begin."

Following Clark's command, Billy Strivectin and I walked slowly across the gray cement locker room floor. We sat down on one of the twenty-long wooden benches, which hugged the freshly painted *blue* cement walls and gray metal lockers. I purposely sat beside Big John McKinney Melville's veteran right tackle because he smiled while all the others looked away. Billy quickly sat beside me to my right.

"Ok, let's do a recap. First, you senior *band boys* walk in here *late*. That's enough to have you both hung by the neck from the tallest tree until dead. And then you both talk like you've never heard of Vince *Lombardi or Lombardi Time*. That is damn insulting. Practically everyone alive has heard of Vince Lombardi and Lombardi Time. Why, just for that alone, you ought to be shot by a firing squad at sunrise without a blindfold. Vince Lombardi is a legend in his own time. Because you two do not know this fact is football sacrilege unless you're playing me or you're are a very dumb spy?"

CHAPTER EIGHT
NOTHING TO PROVE

"Get a rope, Coach," Henri said. "Slow down, Henri, if I hung every son-of-a-witch that misunderstands, disappoints, or second guesses me, I would spend the rest of my waking life officiating at reprisal hangings."

"Cut them! Do it! Do it, Coach! Cut them both. Save them from Clark's Hell and the embarrassment of failure because they are not ready, Coach, on day one!"

"Cut them, cut them," the football veterans shouted while Billy and I remained seated and, sadly, feeling unwanted and unloved.

My brother Tom once said:

In order to become a Melville football player, one must develop a high tolerance for verbal and physical abuse. It is part of the football locker room culture.

What psychology made Jim Clark wish to degrade, emasculate, and belittle Melville band boys? Did his self-esteem feel threatened? Having never in my young memory been publicly denigrated in such a foul, flagrant, and demeaning way, this rough experience Clark called *tough love* killed me softly.

So, I took several deep breaths and let them out slowly. While my mind searched for answers, I questioned my actions. Had I challenged his leadership and authority by speaking out? He couldn't stand for that. No leader would have. He had to have the last word and let me, as well as every senior tryout present, know who was in charge. I sensed Clark would only allow one man to have the spotlight. That one man was he.

"But, Henri, here is the thing. They both came in here wearing those Centerville Blue Superman T-shirts, dark naval pilot sunglasses, wild Bermuda shorts, and high-top tennis shoes, and both are carrying the same ridiculously old blue Raggedy Ann gym bags that look like they went through a rummage sale, two World wars, a hail storm, and a goat hanging? Must I always remind you, *band boy,* our school colors are *red*, not Centerville *blue*? We wear scarlet, not blue. Now our job is to take you a bunch of nothing and turn it into a bunch of something. It's not an easy task. It will require hard work, good weather, and a truckload of lucky horseshoes."

"Are you going to send them both packing?" Henri asked. "You will weed out the *quitters,* huh, Coach,*"* Henri said with a sly soft wily smile and a wink implying he and Clark knew something we did not.

"That's right, Captain Henri."

"What about the screw-ups, Coach? There are always a couple of screw-ups."

"From this day forward, I will see to it that you screw-ups will not have the time or excess energy to screw up. You have fifteen weekdays of an intense training regimen ahead of you before our Friday night opener with *La Santos* in three weeks, and you must be ready because they will."

"Henri, we've been through this; you know I have a no-cut policy. Let's let them run in the fun run first and see how they do. Then if they do well, we will see how far they can march. If they pass both of those, there is no need to rush the inevitable. Savor it like a fine French wine, swish it around in your mouth, smell the bouquet and see if it has legs... We will soon see what kind of grape these young green vines grow."

"We'll test their limits?"

"You can be sure of that."

"We'll push them beyond what they thought possible, right?"

"Yes, of course. We'll soon learn more about them than they want us to know. We'll soon know whether they have the right stuff."

"When will we start?"

"After the school clock strikes twelve, *Lombardi Time*? The hot temperatures forecast will make it very rough on everyone out there today."

While they discussed the *suffering* we were expected to endure as a result of today's hot Missouri weather, forecast my mind wondered. I remembered in the *musical Camelot* what King Arthur sang about the *pleasant weather* in Camelot:

Arthur

It's true! It's true! The crown has made it clear.

The climate must be perfect all year.

A law was made a distant moon ago here:

July and August cannot be too hot.

And there's a legal limit to the snow here

In Camelot.

The winter is forbidden till December

And exits March the second on the dot.

By order, summer lingers through September

In Camelot.

Camelot! Camelot!

In short, there's simply notA more congenial spot

For happily-ever-after, than here

In Camelot.

Then at the end of the play, I heard this my favorite part:

Don't let it be forgot

That once there was a spot

For one brief shining moment

That was known as Camelot

Camelot {The Musical) 1960

Billy and I expected a more congenial spot. We expected acceptance, encouragement, and happily ever after, but we found degradation, emasculation, and belittlement. I had never experienced such harsh verbal abuse. It chipped away at the heart and soul in me and stomped on my pride as I suspected it did to Billy also. I wondered how many young band boys Jim Clark and Captain Paul Henri had blatantly diminished. Whose faces flushed red and whose cheeks wet with tears of pride less shame? I wondered why my deceased father, John Cameron, would want me to play football for this man from a bygone football era when they didn't wear a face mask. I wondered why anyone would willingly put themselves through this. I wondered what possible lessons my father wanted me to learn from this clueless, classless old-school football coach.

Billy said. "Two years ago, my brother Tom tried out as a senior band member for Jim Clark's Melville football team. He was also harassed due to his band connection, but he stuck it out. He made the first team at quarterback. Through hard work, determination, and natural ability, he won the Golden Helmet award and a beautiful four-year full-ride football scholarship to the University of Missouri.

"Yes, that's right, Billy, go on."

"And now you have an intense need to succeed no matter what? Don't you, deep down in your gut, don't you, Cam?"

"Well, yes. Ok. So?"

"Recently, Melville's Bret Hart wrote an interesting article on that very subject. You probably read it."

I felt uneasy. I shuffled on my bench seat. I wondered where this was going with this.

"What is your point? What's this all about, Billy?"

"Well, it's this. You probably see yourself scoring touchdowns with ease, like your father, John the Scott Cameron, did and your brother Tom did two years ago, am I right?"

"Yes, sure, you're right."

"And now you've received his letter. In it, he requested that you play football here at Melville.

I shook my head, yes, but my stomach felt uneasy.

"Ok, what's your point, Billy?"

My mission was clear, to try out for his football team at quarterback, win the Golden Helmet and become a Melville man like my father requested but not for vanity, personal glory, or fame, to get a girlfriend, or to impress, or play solely for self-promotion, as Clark suggested. But to honor my deceased war hero father's last dying request for Tom and me.

"With all due respect, Cam and I mean you no harm, but may I suggest, no, may I strongly suggest, a better, more prudent course of action to be followed here?"

"Yes, sure, shoot. Billy, I'm always open to suggestions and a better, more prudent course of action. Who isn't?"

"Well, now that I have your strict attention, I suggest, no, I strongly suggest, that you stand up now, walk over to the hallway water fountain and take a long cool refreshing drink of cold water. Splash a little on your face. Then wait until your burning desire to play Melville football for Coach Jim Clark goes away, like a horrible bad dream that will soon become a nightmare if you stay. Then after it goes away, run, do not walk to the nearest exit. You must reassess this noxious quest to succeed at Melville football, Cam."

A lesser motivated young man, I suppose, would have followed Billie's sound advice and run out of there, filled with self-righteous indignation and just cause. Yes, we band boys had been treated shabbily by the varsity football players for years. As you might expect, a few of the younger players were now starting to mimic that bad behavior. Monkey see, monkey, do I suppose?

While Clark continued to speak about the importance of maintaining Melville's winning tradition and how we had disrespected our red school colors, dressed as we were, in Centerville blue, Billy Strive tin whispered.

"Listen to me, Cam; I'm serious. I beg you. Do not attempt to follow in your brother Tom's and your deceased father, John Cameron's footsteps. Do not follow your father's dream for you and their successes. It's a fool's errand. Follow your own dream. Follow your *bliss*!"

Following your bliss was the philosophy of that early sixties era.

"How do I follow my bliss, Billy? When sometimes life is a piece of…."

"Listen, Cam; you do not have to be like them or do as they did. You do not have to follow in their large footsteps. Chart your own course. Set your own heading. Be the Captain of your ship. Be who you are, not who he wants you to be. Get yourself free—no need to discuss this. Pick up your old blue hand-me-down gym bag and say Haste La Vista, Adios amigos. You have *nothing to prove* here, Cam, nothing."

"Nothing to prove, nothing to prove. Would you have me abandon my war hero father's last dying request of me, Billy? Should I throw away his army uniform and his medals too? What about his golden Helmet? It sits on the mantle, taunting me. Erase my connection? What else would you have me abandon, Billy?"

"Nothing else; simply return to the band where you belong and do what comes naturally. You're following a ghost's dream seeking a ghost's approval. This is not your goal. It's your my deceased father's goal for you?"

I could have used Clark's bad behavior toward me today as an excuse to retreat-which is just another word for quitting-and feel justified in doing so.

My brother Tom said:

Some things in life a man must do which you may not enjoy, but you must endure when prudence says, run away fast. It takes a special kind of bravery and courage to try out, stay and play Melville football. Only a few survive the harsh physical training program that Jim Clark administers, and even fewer play. But if you stay, playing Melville football will make you stronger if you can push through the pain.

Torn between two choices, I realized this insurmountable mission of becoming a Melville Man-not totally of my own choosing- would not be easy, if not nearly impossible, to achieve. I needed to make it through the tough training program Jim Clark administered.

"Life is perplexing, Billie. There are too many choices."

"Follow your bliss, Cam, not someone else's. Find your passion and follow."

Billy continued.

"Melville football kills guys like us. Boys like us need to face up to that truth. We are artists. We're musicians; we're sensitive, weak, and, yes, sometimes pathetic. We seek and need psychological help. We're not warriors; we don't carry the tough warrior gene. We'll never be strong, not like them. I can't wait to graduate and leave this crazy, upside-down football town. Well, those are the cold hard facts, my friend. Heed my warnings or not."

"Why are you trying out for the team if you think like that, Billy?"

"When I decided to try out for the Melville Football Team, I hadn't considered, nor factored in, the *'Clark factor.'*

"Tom says football will make us stronger, Billy; it will. It did Tom, and it did my father! He said so in his War Letter."

"No, football won't make us stronger. That belief is a myth, a fallacy, used repeatedly to suck you in. It promises an outcome that cannot be. We are only fooling *ourselves*. Over the years, many nearly died in Clark's Hell, you know.

I shifted my weight and heard Clark shout loudly.

"Laxly!"

"Yes, Coach."

"What is all that loud bussing about over there? It sounds like a nest of yellow jackets. Why I can't even hear myself think."

"Coach Clark, you know my name is not Laxly. It's *Lax Exley,* and I'm sitting over here beside the two band boys who just sat down.

"Yes, but what are they discussing? Do they think it is more important than what I'm saying?"

"They're discussing whether or not your coaching style will make them stronger; Billy thinks it won't, Cameron thinks it might."

"What do you think, Exley?"

"I will not enter that land-mined conversation, Coach."

"Why not?"

Fools rush in where wise men fear to tread.

Lax quoted these song lyrics from a 1940 Frank Sinatra song titled: *Fools Rush In.*

"What does that mean? What does that mean?"

"It means if I'm smart, I will not rush in to give an opinion on this Coach."

"Exley?

"Yeah, Coach."

"Take a memo."

"Take a memo about what, Coach?"

"Baseball, that's what."

"Ah, baseball, the all-American sport I love?"

"That's right, baseball. That's *one strike* on Cameron and Strive tin."

"So, what happens after *two strikes,* Coach?"

"Why after strike two, they'll go stand on the corner."

"Stand on what corner, Sir?"

"Why the two corners of *Liberty and Freedom.*"

"In downtown Melville?"

"Yes."

"And what will they do while standing on those two corners of *Liberty and Freedom*, Sir."

"Watch all those pretty Melville girls go by. Breathe in the fresh air, enjoy the day, and be very grateful some patriots gave their full measure of devotion so they can stand on those two corners anywhere in America."

"But you don't allow a Melville man *to fraternize with any girls during football season, Coach.*"

"Yes, that's right, I don't. But you can still read from the menu if you can't order the meal."

"But what happens after strike three, Coach?" Lax Exley seemed concerned.

"Well, in baseball parlance, *after three strikes, you're out*. You lower your head, kick the dirt, throw your bat against the backstop with disgust and remove yourself from the field. Hell boys, these are the best years of your life."

I turned and nudged Big John.

"Did Coach Clark just say, 'these are the best years of our life'?

"No, he said, '*may you die in the arms of another man's wife, Steven Mandrake Cameron.* Big John said, smiling.

"What? How do you know my middle name is *Mandrake?*"

"I'm not a potted plant around here, you know. I see all. I know all. I'm the Melville Times newspaper boy. I know every clean and every dirty little secret in Melville because the night has a thousand eyes, and I have a thousand spies."

"Who are they?"

"For starters, the football Mother's Club, my Irish mum is the president, you know. Your parents pulled your middle name from the popular syndicated comic strip, *Mandrake, the magician.*

"Aren't you in contention with Lax Exley as valedictorian, Big John? They usually pass over you football players.

"We both have name recognition. Last year Donald Duck got twenty-one votes, and Goofy got eleven. Its name recognition usually wins these contests at Melville." Big John said.

"Plus, the fact that my father is the town doctor and his mother owns half of the town helps. We were not picked on our merit but on our family names, sadly to say." Lax said.

"But being the class president must be rewarding, Lax?"

"Yes, it is an honor, but I never imagined what they expect of me. It's a lot of pressure placed on this young boy's shoulders, and sometimes I feel I'm about ready to *crack*." Lax said.

 Clark overheard.

"I hear what you are saying, Exley. I know exactly how you feel. They're still trying to get an extra smile out of this old pack mule, you know."

Clark held his gaze. Lax shifted in his seat uneasily.

"Exley, do I see long hair covering your ears, son, stand up and turn around.

"Well, maybe a little strand or two by your standards, Coach, but I think it only needs a *slight trim*."

"A slight trim hell, it looks like a duck's butt. What is that haircut called?"

"It is called a DA, Coach. It's all the rage today."

"No good self-respecting Melville football player would wear long hair that looks like a duck's rear."

"Well, yes, sir, certainly nobody wants a haircut to look like a duck's rump, that is for sure, but don't you remember Sampson's long hair, Coach? His Long hair gave him strength. I suppose he was the strongest man on earth at that time."

"Yes, but do you remember how he lost all of his strength, Exley?"

"Yes, sure, everyone knows Delilah cut Sampson's long hair, but with all due respect to you, Coach, our senior class advisor and physics teacher, Phil Gleeson is the smartest man I know, and he says there's no correlation between being an effective athlete and the length of one's hair!"

"If ole Willy Gleeson is so damn smart, Exley, why isn't he rich? Exley, be first in line for haircuts tomorrow morning, or I'll shear you myself. And Exley?"

"Yes, sir,

"There is more to this haircut rule than you may be aware of. You should know this after three years of dodging it. We're trying to build a team here, a team where no one man stands out above the other or stands alone. When you join this football team, all of your long hair is left on the locker room floor. The goal is for all of you to look alike. Your *individualism must be shed. It must be sacrificed for the good of the team, the collective*! There is more to this haircut rule than you are aware of, Exley."

Strangely, I thought this old coach was quoting Carl Marx or Lenin. His idea of training us to be rugged individuals dependent on no one seemed to conflict with Clark's goal of working for the sake of *Clark's team*. I would not expect Clark's team to work for my sake. Clearly, I would need to spend more time on this or maybe discuss this with my brother Tom.

Clark spoke to us about a summer training letter.

CHAPTER NINE
TRAINING LETTER

"I hope every one of you lads did what we expected of you over the summer."

Big John reacted.

"Whoa, wait a sec back that mail train up, Coach. What were *we lads* expected to do over the summer, Coach?" Big John McKinney asked, his voice a weak whisper, which was his customary manner.

Didn't you get the summer *training letter* we mailed out to everyone in early June, Big John?"

"No, Coach."

"What? Did anyone here receive our summer training letter?"

"No, Coach." The ten football veterans answered.

"Damn! If you want something done right, you had better do it yourself. I can do the work of two men but not three. My three assistants always prepare and mail those letters out, and none got through."

"Maybe you need to return to the old Missouri Pony Express days, Coach. They always got the mail through in all kinds of weather and were always on time." Captain Henri said.

"What do you know about the Pony Express, Captain Henri?"

"Well, I know the Pony Express started in St. Joseph, Missouri. The young riders were tough and light of weight, and they rode day and night through hostile Indian Territory with both guns blazing. They stopped only to pick up a fresh horse about every ten miles. They rode across the Great Plains and over the Rocky Mountains to Sacramento, California. Those were the exciting days of yesteryear, Coach."

"Those are bedtime stories and folklore from the old wild west, Captain Henri. Yes, they rode through hostile Indian Territory and cut the time to deliver a five-cent letter from one and a half weeks to eight days, but not with both guns blazing. They only carried one gun to save weight in order to carry more mail. But we digress. Captain Henri, what can we expect from you and this year's Melville football squad?"

"We are young, tough, and brave like those Pony Express boys. And we will come together as a team this year, Coach. I promise." Paul Henri said.

"Perhaps one should not promise anything they can't deliver on. I 've heard nothing but promises and excuses from this team for the last two years. I'm tired and disgruntled. Melville supporters are tired and disgruntled. A stirred, disgruntled fan will turn against you. I've seen it. They want us to *win* Henri, *not tie* Centerville. And the way to our success is to do what, Henri."

"Practice harder than our opponents."

Clark turned quickly to face the portable chalkboard. He picked up the chalk and wrote this.

'Practice makes you perfect.' Vince Lombardi.

"Coach Clark quoted Vince Lombardi's quote wrong, Big John," I whispered.

"What?"

"He quoted that famous Vince Lombardi quote wrong. Should I tell him?"

Big John turned quickly. He spoke to me sternly.

"No, don't say anything. If you raise your hand, Cameron, I will break your arm."

I quickly pulled my hand down at the thought, but it was *too late*.

"Did I see a hand go up? What is it, Cameron? What could you possibly add to a perfect Vince Lombardi quote?"

"Well, ah, I believe you've mistakenly written *Mr. Vince Lombardi's* famous quote wrong, Coach?"

"What? What? Wrong?"

Jim Clark recoiled as if shot by a high-powered rifle bullet.

"I believe *Mr. Lombardi* never said, *'practice makes you perfect,* Coach.'

I recognized this famous Lombardi quote from the large Vince Lombardi poster, which covered my Brother Tom's upstairs bedroom door.

"I believe *Mr. Lombardi* said, *'perfect practice makes perfect.'*

"Cameron, are you playing with me? Because if you are playing me, son, there will be hell to pay. Laxly, is he playing with me?"

"No, Coach, He doesn't know much about Vince Lombardi, and what he does know is mush. Pay him no mind."

The team laughed. But Clark didn't laugh. The laughter didn't suit his serious nature and old-school ideas and philosophy of coaching. I found he did not take well to being corrected. Clark gave me an angry glare, the cold kind you'd never want to be directed at you. In his wildest dreams, he never thought he had quoted his hero, Coach Vince Lombardi, wrong, but he had.

"I don't suffer fools gladly, Cameron," Clark said.

I thought Clark was now quoting Shakespeare, from King Lear, or maybe Macbeth. Could it be?

"Cameron, how do you know my Lombardi quote is wrong?"

"I read it on a poster."

"You read it on a poster!"

"Yes, sir."

Clark made a quick pivot. He turned, picked up an eraser from the chalkboard, and erased the quote. He rewrote the correct quote on the blackboard. When finished, Clark then turned around and continued talking to us.

Clark spoke next about his three assistants.

"My three stout-hearted assistants and I will attempt to teach you lads *respect* for this great game and the rules of sportsmanship, as well as teach you the *skills* necessary to be a fine football player. This we promise. Every part of your soul and character will be transformed and re-landscaped. That is our goal. This is our mission."

My eyes searched the locker room to find *those three stout-hearted assistant Coaches* of which he spoke, those landscapers of our character, those phantoms of the opera, those three mysterious men that would teach us life's lessons and reveal our character and take us to a higher level never seen or experienced before. Still, there were none present, and I wondered why. Had it become an insider's secret? If so, a secret I want to crack now.

I nudged Big John.

"Who is Clark's three stout-hearted assistants?" I whispered.

"Shh, I'll tell you later."

"No, tell me now."

"No."

"Yes."

"No."

"Yes."

"I said I'll tell you later, and that is that. Now be quiet. Coach is talking. And don't raise your hand again, or I'll break it, I promise."

"tell me now, or I'll continue to talk. I'll ask him questions and interrupt Clark. I'll…"

"Stop it; you are giving me a headache."

"Tell me, tell me now."

The big tackle leaned forward and held his large hands to his forehead."

"Ok, ok, but no more jabber talk. Clark and Thorn and the two assistants had a little minor altercation." He whispered.

"What minor altercation, Big John?"

"I can't tell you that part. Nobody talks about it."

"You can tell me. I won't talk about it. I'm nobody, remember?"

"Ok, I'll tell you now, but you have to keep it quiet. Coach Clark had a minor altercation with his two assistant coaches, mostly Coach Gary Thorn."

"What minor altercation?"

"Clark would not take back his *'eleven words.'*

"Clark would not take back what *'eleven words?'*"

Big John leaned in closer and whispered these *eleven words*. "*Get the hell out of here, and don't ever come back!*"

"Oh, you neglected to tell me that part."

"Yeah, well...now you know."

Clark asked this question.

"You ten veterans seated here can't hide, and you can't *fake*, your level of physical fitness. You were expected to show up fit and ready. This year's endurance march and senior Fun Run will test that question."

"Viva the Fun Run! Viva Clark's hell! Paul Henri shouted with obvious anticipation. "Bring it on. Let the Fun Run begin, Coach."

"If anyone sitting here is uncertain, they may not have what it takes and has serious doubts about making this year's Melville football team or completing what Bret Hart calls *Clark's Hell,* and the Fun Run to Nowheres, please stand now."

Drum major Billy Strive tin stood tall and all alone.

"You stood, Billy. Are you afraid you do not have the right stuff, son?"

"Yes, sir, I feel out of place here. This varsity football gig is a little overwhelming, Coach, you know."

"Take a couple of deep breaths, son. Your face looks flushed. You may be hyperventilating."

Billy took two deep breaths. He clutched his old blue gym bag in his left hand and pulled it tight to his chest.

"There's is no disgrace in not making this team, son. It takes a strong individual to play this game."

"I know, but I fear I don't have the endurance necessary to finish today's Fun Run and your long death march, Coach."

Captain Henri stood, gritted his teeth, and thrust out his chiseled chin.

"We have *the guts* to get through the Fun Run and *Clark's Hell* again this year, Coach, so *bring it on!*"

To my surprise, Clark ignored Captain Henri's confident bravado and seemed to want something more from this band boy named Billy Strive tin.

"Our job here, as coaches, Billy, is to push, prod, and challenge you until you reach your God-given potential. Can you give that a go?"

"Well, I'm not sure, Coach. You've set the bar exceptionally high, you know. I'm probably not physically or emotionally tough enough to play at the high level you require. For me to make this team, I would have to lower the bar and even the playing field. This would lower your standard for excellence, something I understand you'll never do."

"Well, Billy, if you don't raise the bar, you'll never be challenged sufficiently to improve. Numerous educational studies support that. We do not lower our expectations here; we raise them."

"Could you lower your expectations for me, Coach, this one time until I catch up, just this once?"

"No, we won't lower our expectations, Billy. We won't water them down to even the playing field; doing so impedes your progress. It's like saying mediocrity is ok."

"If I stay, what can I expect, Coach, more failure? Better for me to walk off now and call it a day. Not everyone is cut out for this aggressive warrior sport." Billy said.

"Yes, it's true this game is rough, and it is true your future is uncertain in our warrior domain, and success is not guaranteed, but if you stay, you won't be coddled. We believe those who coddle you are hurting you the most. In our program, you won't receive a lot of hugs, and you definitely will not receive a lot of praise. Too much praise handed out too freely sets up a feeling of false accomplishment. We believe you have no incentive to improve if you're told you're good when you're not. Mediocrity sets in. Nothing ruins a good man more than having someone tell them they are good when they are not. They start to believe it and quit striving to improve. Don't you see that? Too many pats on the back will set you back."

"What if I'm not the hero type, Coach? What if I don't have the skills, the talent, or the confidence to play this rugged team sport?"

"If there's one trait all great Melville football players share, it's self-confidence. When the football game is close, and chaos is all around them, and in the heat of battle, when the moment of truth comes, there is a calmness about them. They *want football*. I've seen it. It's amazing. They thrive on pressure and react without hesitation, filled with self-confidence. It is in those moments if successful; they become a *hero*."

"But Coach, what if I don't have the self-confidence."

Billy stood tall and said his truth honestly. I admired him for that. I remembered what William Shakespeare wrote:

'To thine own self be true,
And it must follow,
As the night the day,
Thou canst not be false to any man.
"And Jesus said in John 8:32:
'And you shall know the truth
And the truth will set you free.'
This much I knew. In that one single instance, their dynamic cross-purposes had surfaced, if only for a moment. Clark felt with effort; Billy could take a wooden Indian nickel and turn it into a silver dollar. Billy thought a wooden nickel could *never* be turned into a silver dollar no matter what amount of effort."

"Can I ask you a personal question?"

"Sure."

"Do you have a girlfriend, Billy?"

"No, sir."

"Why not? You're good-looking enough. So, what are you waiting for, a gold-plated invitation? Do you think some girl will see you walk up and ask you out?

"No, sir."

"Do you date anyone?'

"I like a girl in the band."

"What's her name?"

"Angel."

"Is she honest and trustworthy?"

"Very much so."

"Then what are you waiting for an invitation?"

Clark quoted this old English proverb pertaining to boldness:

"Feint heart never won fair lady.'

"I know, Coach, I know. I'm very shy, but where do we go from here, Coach? We seem to be at a crossroads." Billy said.

"A crossroads, Billy; how so?"

"I think lots of boys like me want to be a Melville football player, but we lack that something you call desire and heart. I know it takes a ton of courage and self-confidence, and a willingness to work hard to play Melville football. Everyone knows you must show up fully conditioned on day one! The truth is almost no one except Maybe Captain Henri here and your veterans want to do the hard training, attend the difficult three-a-day practices, and adhere to the strict discipline code required to excel at this exceedingly violent and aggressive combat sport."

"Have you considered that?" Clark asked Billy. Clark had also guessed correctly. Billy had never been tested, and yes, Billy lacked self-confidence.

"You're in the pursuit of excellence in this manly game. But I'm uncertain, unsure, and frankly afraid that I mightn't have what it takes to succeed. You call that something *the right stuff*."

"There are two kinds of men in this football world, Billy, those who know their limitations and press on and those who know their limitations and will not. If you felt this way, why did you decide to try out for our football team today, Billy?"

"I came here because I love the game of football, and I admire you and your successful football program, Coach. I got caught up in the hype. I wanted to be a part of it, but fear sat on my shoulders constantly. Have you ever been afraid, Coach? I mean, wet your pants, afraid."

"Yes, a time or two or twenty, mostly on the Bataan and in that dreadful death camp. During those scary moments, you will discover who you are, Billy, and what your limits are. Would you like to learn more about yourself, Billy?"

CHAPTER TEN
GOD BLESS AMERICA

Billy thought hard before answering Clark. "I find self-introspection can also be very scary. I'm sorry, Coach, for taking your time, but I can't fake it. I'm not good enough."

"I like your honesty, Billy. But when the weather turns colder, the pucker factor sets in, and you are faced with a test of your team spirit and loyalty. Will you fold like a good book at the end, or will you give it your best shot for your school, town, and teammates?"

Billy started to walk towards the exit. "Hold on a minute before you fly up and away. It's Strivectin, isn't it?

"Yes, sir, Billy Strivectin. I was named after my father."

"No need to get your bowels in an uproar, Strivectin, Just because you don't like dancing to the music we play. "You must look at the terror and doubt in the eye and not back down. Hold your fire until they get closer. Don't circle your wagons too soon, son. Wait until they attack. Then wait till you see the white of their eyes. Once you have given your all and fought the good fight, you can ride off into the sunset like the cowboys always do in the "B" movies and never return."

Billy stopped and turned quickly to face Clark.

"If I stay, what should I expect, Coach? More failure? Better to walk off now and call it a day."

"If you quit today without trying, you may regret not trying it one time later,

Or remain a yellow-bellied milk-toast coward now and forever? Well, are ya?"

Looking crushed like a tin beer can at a Saturday night Fraternity party Billy turned and sat down beside me. The instant and full influence of his psyche and emotions were still unknown and yet to be discovered. Like a lion cub reared in a sheltered pen with sheep. Billy had never experienced the rages of the wild jungle or the Serengeti, where survival relied on fitness, aggression, and self-reliance. It was kill or be killed. Billy only had a rudimentary knowledge of this horribly physically demanding blood sport called football and a limited understanding of its rules and Clark's core philosophy. But Billy knew his limitations, and he knew Coach Jim Clark would never lower his expectations or even the playing field. I, for one, appreciated Billy's sincerity, honesty, and doubts.

Clark had unveiled and stripped Billy Strivectin publicly for all to see. I did not understand this demanding and harsh treatment. It seemed cruel and insensitive. My brother Tom said: *In the middle of a fight on the field of battle, when those around you are being massacred, you have to become emotionally detached and dispassionate to survive.*

I assumed this was the reason for Clark's sharp attacks. Clark wanted Billy to be more. He wanted Billy to have self-respect. I determined that Jim Clark was not the perfect role model my father wrote to us about in his War Letters.

The ten veterans who watched sat like wide-eyed toads, but none came to Billy's rescue or his defense, not one. But then Billy was not a member of *their* team. He was a *band boy*, the lowest of the low, with his chances of making this year's 1960 football squad closer to zero than ten.

Stunned, Billy couldn't answer. Deeply hurt, Billy held his hands to his face and wept hopelessly. Billy suddenly cried out. "Stop it! I'm not cut out for this blood sport, Coach. I don't want the football; I don't need that pressure. I want to play my music. Stop harassing me."

"When I think about what lies ahead for you, I cringe," Clark said. Discipline is the heart of a well-trained squad but once a coward, always a coward."

I watched the blood rush to Billy's face, turning it red. Billy placed his bent arm on my right shoulder to steady and fortify himself. With this sensitive band, the boy's psyche altered, and his naive seventeen-year-old innocence bruised Billy Strivectin uneasily, but honestly, he spoke his truth. For that, he was publicly shamed and humiliated by Coach Jim Clark.

"Expectations, set to low, Billy, will only produce mediocrity at best. Our country deserves better, don't you think? We have a higher purpose, a larger goal here. I know you can't take a round peg and force it into a square hole. However, it could be the biggest disaster in your life if you fail to stay today and don't give it a go. "This is your critical hour. Don't let untested fears keep you from your goals. Now is the time to seize this moment! I encourage boldness, Billy. Be brave."

"Be brave; this is the land of the free coach," Billy said.

"This will remain the land of free so long as it is the home of the brave." Clark quoted Elmer Davis: But we were born free, 1954.

I like your heart, and I respect your moxie, Billy. I hear you, and a few of the band boys were bullied by this football team?"

"Yes, sir. We are a vast pool of easy targets, and it is not just us band boys. It is also the band girls. They don't discriminate. They bully the band girls in different ways."

"What do you want? An apology? Look, you will not get a bear hug or a french kiss here. Surely you don't expect that?"

"No. I expect no apology."

Instead of being supportive, Clark spoke this altered nursery rhyme about Billy: *'All the kings' horses,*
And all the kings' men,

Could not put Billy Strivectin,
Back together again.'

I knew Billy well. Billy has always wanted to be a Melville football player since he was a young kid on the maple side playgrounds. He loved playing sandlot touch football, and he played well. But Billy had a blood disease called hemophilia. He would bruise and bleed easily, and his blood would not clot. That blood condition prevented him from trying out for any significant contact sport at Melville.

Clark sniffed the air around Billy Strivectin like a blue tick bloodhound.

"I can smell a *quitter, you know*."

"What does a quitter smell like, Coach?' Big John asked.

"A quitter has a nasty musty *smell* like an old wet dog. Can you smell a quitter, Big John?"

"No, I can't smell anything from over here, Coach. I used Mennen *After Shave* this morning. That stuff is strong but good."

"I believe in the Clark Theorem-that says quitters know when they will quit. Do you believe that, Strivectin?"

"Well, I never thought about it, Coach, but if you say so," Billy replied.

Clark moved slowly back to the center of the locker room.

"When you think we ask too much of you, take a good look at the training methods of the Spartans. No warriors have ever trained more, in harsher conditions, from birth through maturity. Our methods pale by comparison."

"All for one and one for all, huh, Coach?" Captain Henri said.

Jim Clark spun around to face Henri. His jaws tightened. His face reddened.

"That only works when everyone sacrifices and has skin in the game, not just a few, like you, Captain Henri. Everyone must contribute, not just one man or two or three. We will soon see if you lads are enthusiastic about uniting as one. We will see if you can become a musketeer."

I heard footsteps. We all looked up at once. I recognized him.

"Mike Carson, please don't tell me you are coming in here late again with another lame excuse?"

"Well, I'm sorry, Coach. I hope you don't mind my being *a little late* for your first-morning brief for seniors. But my bicycle tire leaked the back tire. My dog hid the patch can. I had to run here. See, I'm all out of breath."

"Being *a little late* is like being a little pregnant, Mike. Of course, I mind. Darn, your lazy hide anyway, Mike. I loathe and despise tardiness with every fiber of my being. Do you want to be known as the fellow who always arrives late, Mike?"

"Not unless it's my funeral, Coach!"

"Do you have a different set of rules for the football manager than you do the band boys?" Billy asked. "What's the deal here, Coach?"

Clark pivoted quickly. "No, I haven't different rules, but there are always a few young men every year who think my restrictions don't apply to them. They think they're special. They have no self-discipline. They are full of arrogance and self-centeredness. They think this world owes them something. I take all infractions of our team rules seriously. Yes, I do. If you had tried out three years earlier, like every veteran seated here, you would know that, Strivectin.

Billy Strivectin leaned in close and said this.

"What the band boys really want, Cam, is to have this coach *respect us*, not denigrate us scare the pee out of us, and make us wet our pants as I did."

Clark's head turned quickly as his voice rose.

"Mike?"

"Yeah, Coach?"

"Mike, why are you standing over by my office door, cussing? A man who cusses is a man who has a weak vocabulary."

"I'm putting your four, brand new, out of the box, Spalding game footballs you laid out into this tight-fitting yellow mesh bag. I mean golden mesh bag for the *iron man competition* later today, Coach."

"Mike, did someone just run out of this locker room in a blur?"

"It looked like a senior to me, Coach."

"A senior?"

"Yes, I think so."

A senior walk on?"

"Yes, sir."

"A senior walk-on, with no football experience, from Milo Clem's award-winning Melville band?"

"I think so."

"Wearing that damn Centerville blue Superman T-shirt and carrying an old torn blue gym bag?"

"Yes, sir."

"Is he a darn quitter, Mike?"

"Well, Coach, he ran out of your locker room. I would say that makes him a quitter and qualifies him as our first team casualty for this season."

"Do you know him personally, Mike?"

"No, Coach, not personally!"

"You mean you have a fellow student, a classmate, and a Melville band member carrying a torn gym bag and wearing a damn Centerville blue Superman T-shirt in our sacred Melville locker room, and you don't know him?"

"I don't associate with the Melville *band boys,* you know."

"What! Why Mike?"

"They are geeks."

"They are the Greeks?"

"No sir, they are the Geeks. You know, strange and nerdy and most likely to become rich."

"By God, somebody here ought to know him personally, Mike. He just flew out of our locker room. Go get him, Mike. You do not run out of our sacred locker room and not say why. Does anyone here know where he lives? Does anybody here know where that darn quitter lives?"

I raised my hand before Big Jim's face could form another scowl.

"It was Billy Strivectin, Coach."

"Is he a quitter, Cameron?"

"Well, I guess so, now, after he..."

"I don't like the tone of your voice. Do you think I made this band boy quit?

I shook my head yes.

"You have a lot to learn about quitters, Cameron. No one quits because of someone or something someone else said or did. That is what they will tell you. Quitting is something they want to do. They use any excuse to make it seem justified. Where does this quitter live? Unravel this puzzle quickly, Cameron."

"Well, Billy lives on 44 Maple Street, down by the playground and the photo lab, besides Mr. Saperstein's bakery, where my grandmother Helmick and Mrs. Bittner bake those fresh German Bee Sting cakes and fruit pies."

"Tell me more about Band Boy Billy, Cameron."

"Tell you more? Ok. Well, he is different but not weird different. He loves crossword puzzles, and miniature golf, runs three miles daily and is reclusive and nonsocial. He's a real introvert but very smart. He loves action-adventure radio shows like the Green Hornet and reads superhero comic books like Superman, Batman, and Robin. He collects comic books and *baseball cards*."

"Why in the world would anyone save those old comic books and bubble gum baseball player's cards? Do you know, Cameron?"

"Billy says that someday his pristine superhero comic book collection and baseball card collection will be worth a small fortune. Go figure!"

"Which ball players does he save?"

"He favors the great New York Yankee hitters. Babe, Joe, Yogi, Mickey, Roger, and the boys."

Clark turned.

"How long did this *band boy* last, Mike?"

"Ten minutes and twenty-five seconds by my crude calculations, Coach. But remember, I arrived a little late."

"Don't remind me. He's the lucky one, you know, Mike."

"Why, Coach?'

"Staying and playing takes a mindset that says I will succeed no matter what. Few men have it. When I see it, I'm in awe. We're sorry to report that Billy Strivectin lacked the conviction and the warrior ethos necessary to succeed. Billy gave up before being truly tested.

I remembered what Thomas Alva Edison once said about giving up too soon:

Many of life's failures are people who did not realize how close they were to success when they gave up...

"Go find him now, Mike, and bring him back to me hog-tied, if need be. We might salvage him yet and save him from his self-defeating thinking."

"Yes, sir. Yes, sir, I'm on it."

"And check that quitter out. See if he is a *spy* sent by Gary Thorn to spy on us to find our strength and depth. Find out, Mike and bring him back to me immediately, do you hear?"

"And Mike...

"Yes, Coach."

"When you return, bring back my red bull horn from the football equipment room closet, top shelf. Now hurry before he gets away."

Soon Mike Carson returned breathlessly. He handed Clark his red bullhorn, and Clark carefully laid it face down on the cement floor at his own feet.

"What took you so darn long, Mike? Did you stop on the way to sneak a smoke? How many times have I told you the perils of cigarette smoking?"

"Coach, you know you don't allow anyone in your Melville football program to smoke."

"Did you find him, Mike? Did you find that yellow-bellied quitter? Did you scalp him or hog-tie him? Did you bring Superman back alive, kicking and screaming?"

"No, Coach."

"No! Why not Mike?"

"He ran away fast, really fast. Who would have thought a member of ole Milo Clem's award-winning Melville band could run that fast for that long?"

"Fast! Strivectin can run fast, Mike?"

"Yes, very fast, Coach, and he carried that old gym bag under his arm like a football or a loaf of bread. He is very strong and powerful."

"Faster than a speeding bullet; more powerful than a locomotive; able to leap tall buildings in a single bound; and can bend steel with his bare hands."

"What?"

"Did Srivectin come out of a phone booth Mike, and did someone in the crowd say, 'Look up in the sky? It's a bird. It's a plane. No, it's Superman'."

"No, Coach, why?"

"Then it wasn't Superman."

"Why not?"

"Superman always ducks into a phone booth to change from Clark Kent into Superman."

The team and I laughed loud. This was the first time I saw Clark laugh. Clark finally showed me he had a sense of humor.

"How do you know all of that about Superman, Coach? I asked.

"We bought a new Motorola black television to replace the small round Sylvania black, the first television set my wife and I ever owned. We watch Superman and the Kate Smith Show every afternoon. I especially love that beautiful Irving Berlin song <u>God Bless America</u>."

The following was part of the lyrics of that great Irving Berlin song <u>God Bless America</u> that Kate Smith sang:

While *the storm clouds gather from across the sea,*
 Let us swear allegiance to a land that is free,
 Let us all be grateful for a land so fair,
As we raise our voices in solemn prayer.
 God bless America,
Land that I love.
Stand beside her, and guide her
Thru the night, with a light from above
From the mountains to the prairies,

To the oceans, white with foam
God bless America, my home sweet home.'

"I, too, like that <u>God Bless America</u> song, Mr. Clark. But it gave me cold chills in the last stanza."

"It gives everyone cold chills in the last stanza."

Clark's eyes caught Ronnie Dudiaks. Clark stopped.

"You have been unusually quiet this morning Ronnie Dudiak. Have you been out staying up late?"

"No, sir."

"Well, your eyes look red, and they say the eyes are the portal to the soul. Are you suffering from a hangover, son?"

"No, Coach, you know you don't allow us to drink alcoholic drinks. You have a very strict, no-nonsense temperance policy.

The veterans chuckled.

"You're darn right I do! Alcohol and sports don't mix. If you never jump on that wagon, you'll never have to worry about falling off it. Not everyone can handle alcohol, Ronnie. Some day they might figure out why. If you want to avoid trouble, say no to alcohol. Look, each year, we set team and personal goals. Tell me, what's your *personal goal* for this football season, Ronnie?"

"Well, I hope to beat the Melville reception record of seven touchdowns in one game, Coach, set back in '41' by 'Two Fingers' Gerry Lee Meeks, the part half Irish and half Cherokee Indian and all district left-end.

"That's one lofty goal, Ronnie. Three things can happen when we put the football into the air Ronnie. Two of them are bad. What are they?"

"The pass can be incomplete, wasting a down, or intercepted, Coach."

"That's right, but only one of the three has a successful outcome. Is that not also true, Ronnie?"

"Yes, sure, it's true, it's' caught. But sometimes I think you have to take a what-the-hell attitude, Coach, and go with the philosophy of nothing ventured, nothing gained. I mean, what's life without a little gamble?

"Big risk, big reward philosophy. That is a gambler's philosophy, for sure, Ronnie. That sounds like Gary Thorn, and you're Dad talking to me now. In gambling, there is always the element of luck. I believe we make our own luck Ronnie with our strong effort and good choices. One follows the other. Good choices bring good results. In sports, we measure a team's success by the number of points they put on the scoreboard, not by the number of big risks they take during the game. What does your Dad say?"

"My Dad says you rely on ball control too much. He says your offense should pass the football more, Coach."

"Yeah, I know what Carl says, but if you live by the *pass,* you die by the pass. The forward pass was a historical breakthrough, a real game changer, Ronnie. No one ever thought of going over the heads of their opponent's defensive formation before. It *caught* on. No pun intended."

"None took, Coach."

"That single innovation changed the game. A very clever football coach thought of that. But in football and war, the ground game will always be king. Control the ground, and you control the battlefield. How is your Dad, Ronnie? Does he still hold a grudge against me?"

"Well, yes, of course, my Dad still holds a grudge against you, Coach. That will never change."

Big John whispered to me.

"So does Gary Thorn and his three assistants."

"Well, like my grandpappy Bo Clark said.

'Keep your friends close and your enemy's closer. If you are going to have an enemy, you might as well have a powerful enemy. What else does Carl Dudiak, the Board of Education President say about me now, Ronnie? Tell me the truth now. Tell me something I've not already heard, and please don't sugarcoat it, Ronnie."

"My Dad says you're a self-centered, arrogant, egotistical, win at all costs, three yards and a cloud of dust, old school football Coach. My Dad says you will kill someone someday, and you ought to be fired before that happens, and when given the opportunity, he will do it. But the most difficult concept for him to grasp, Coach, is your absurd willingness to put us through *Clark's*

Hell the first day in full gear. Every sane football Coach in Missouri believes we should take it slow and easy in our first several sessions before passing out the pads, helmets, and uniforms."

"Is that all he said, Ronnie? Are you sure you didn't leave anything out? That barely scratches the front bumper."

"My Dad says when you win a football game, you walk around like a proud peacock strutting his feathers. Dad says *you are a veteran's parade all by yourself, and you think you're God's gift to football, but in reality, you are as destined to win* Melville football as a wood stove is in Hawaii."

"You're getting better."

"Look, Coach, everyone knows my Dad claims that his youth league team, the patriots, is really what makes your football teams successful. He says all eleven senior veterans on this season's football team rooster have played for and coached by my Dad in the youth league."

"Ronnie."

"Yeah, Coach?"

"Next time, sugarcoat it for me."

"That was sugarcoated, Coach. I said, heck Dad, everyone knows that. If you take away your strong feeder system, Dad, then Coach Clark will become just another Joe trying hard to make a five hundred season. I said all of that, of course, to keep him quiet, Coach. No slight intended."

"None took, Ronnie! So, your Dad says I push players too hard at the outset of the season. Is that his argument?"

"Pretty much, but he basically disagrees with almost everything you do. He says yours is an outdated training philosophy. He says your hay day is over, and your days at Melville are numbered. He says this is *a game* played by boys for fun and comradeship and should be more akin to intramural football. Not that the high power-packed, high-stakes pressurized game that you and your three assistant coaches promote satisfies your own ambition and egos. What do you think about that?"

CHAPTER ELEVEN
FUN RUN TO NOWHERE

"What we have here, Ronnie, are rumors and rumblings from the distant past. A hardy Hi-Ho-Silver and the sound of retreating hoof beats, made from another disgruntled Melville football player *who quit on day one,* as I recall."

"Yes, unfortunately, that's true, Coach. My Dad did quit on the first day. He was exhausted. Like you tell us there are *leaders* and *laggards, I guess Dad was a laggard.*"

"Did you say anything to Carl in my defense, Ronnie?"

"Yeah, sure, Coach. Everyone knows your players are superbly equipped and the best trained in the Missouri Valley Athletic League. Everyone knows we've got to be in top physical condition- on day one- to play football for Jim Clark or don't even try out. You believe *winning is important* on so many levels.

"Well, I believe winning is very important, and here is why. In 24 years of coaching here at Melville High School, I've never had any of the boys who played for me come back and say they were *unhappy* because *they won.* My job is *not to train losers, Ronnie.* I don't want to teach you how to *lose.* I don't want to pass that on as my *legacy.* I want to teach you how to *win.* Why the hell? Our earliest ancestor's survived because they depended on their cunning, courage, stamina, wits, and strength to stay alive. But too few today are willing to take the punishing training necessary to achieve success, Ronnie. They are too quick to drop out, too quick to give up, and too quick to quit. If this sad trend continues, there might come a day when they will applaud the quitter more than the winner, the fellow who sacrifices. They might say it will free them from the difficult task and allow them more time to place toward other, more noble pursuits. I fear an emasculation of our boys. That is why I train you, lads, as hard as I do from the start. My job is to have you ready to make that gallant stand on any battlefield and beachhead anywhere."

Ronnie Dudiak shook his head once again, agreeing.

"I know, Coach. I know.

"My dad says you ask too much of your players."

"Well, did you remind Carl that playing football for Melville is not required? Everyone signs up here of their own free will, Ronnie. No one holds a gun to your head. No one threatens you. There is no coercion here. You are all *volunteers,* and that is what makes you special. We will probably have over one hundred boys try out today, but if I had to go to war today, Ronnie, I couldn't think of a better bunch of boys. I would rather lead into battle than you boys right here."

"I know, Coach, we all feel the same way about you, and we would follow you into *war anytime, anywhere.* I believe I speak for everyone here when I say that it is an honor and a privilege to play football for a successful coach like you, sir."

Ronnie said nothing more.

I got a little choked up, which made me feel fuzzy inside. Tom says, 'Stevie, you're way too sensitive to become a football player, and you had better lose that trait fast.'

Troubled, I turned to face Big John and asked.

Big John, was Ronnie telling the truth?"

"One never knows. Ronnie is prone to embellishment, you know. We call them *Ronnie tales*."

"Then how do you know when Ronnie he is lying."

"When his lips are moving, he is lying." Big John replied.

I heard loud voices. I looked up. About one hundred excited underclass tryouts rush into the small Melville locker room. Coach Clark and Mike Carson moved quickly. They shouted orders. They quickly distributed old practice uniforms and helmets to everyone. To my surprise, Clark fitted each of his *ten senior veterans* with brand-new helmets, but no *new helmet* was handed to me. I wondered why. I walked over to Lax and asked.

"Why won't Clark give me a new helmet like he gave you and all the senior veterans? Does Mr. Clark think I will not be around tomorrow?"

"Yes, probably so," Lax replied.

At exactly eleven forty-five, *Lombardi time,* we took to the black cinder track at the white starting pole, at the fifty-yard line in full uniform. All the underclass tryouts, about one hundred and five I counted, sat in the stands, ready to watch the senior fun run.

I took this opportunity to ask Coach Clark a burning question. I raised my hand slowly while Big Jim predictably scowled with a furrowed brow.

"Coach, do you remember my father when he played quarterback for you before he went off to the war?"

"Vaguely, Cameron."

I wondered why this coach could only vaguely remember possibly being the best quarterback ever to play for Melville High School and the first winner of the prestigious Golden Helmet award for outstanding play. I would pursue this burning question later at a better time.

We jockeyed for a good starting position in the hot blazing sun, which beat down on us like a thousand giant heat lamps, turned on the highest temperature. Clark spoke loud to be heard by all.

"What say you noble sons of Melville? Are you ready for a little Fun run? Are you ready for what the Melville Times News word smith and certifiable nut case, Bret Hart, pen named the *fun Run to Nowhere*?"

Clark smiled and waved to Bret Hart, who sat in the stands. Bret gave Clark a quick hand jester universally recognized in return.

Are we ready, Captain Henri?"

"Yes, I think so, Coach!"

"*You think so?*"

"*I know so!*"

"Are you ready for Clark's Hell?"

"I'm ready for nine kinds of Clark's Hell, Coach."

"Are you ready too, Big John?"

"About as ready as I'll ever be, Coach. I trained every morning with Captain Henri and the boys right after my delivery of the morning newspapers and delivery of a few cases of my white lightning to my buyers. Most of us ran one hundred miles per week in preparation for this first day, Coach."

"Well, that's fine, but you had better curtail your illegal financial enterprise, son. The government revenues don't take kindly to missing out on tax revenue. You don't want to stand between the government tax boys and a revenue enhancer."

"Don't you believe in free enterprise, Coach? Capitalism gives me a reward for my efforts, Coach." Big Jim chuckled to himself at what seemed like an insider's joke.

"You have been lucky so far with that unlawful enterprise of yours, but what happens to you when your luck runs out? What then?"

"Then I'll become another casualty of the American justice system, Coach and a ward of the state, three squares and a cot."

Clark sighed, then turned to face us.

"What you lads are about to experience today will test your courage, stamina, and will. I hope you lads had a pleasant summer. It's over!"

"It's Showtime!" Captain Henri shouted. Big John and Captain Paul Henri began to swivel their hips, singing the latest dance sensation seen on Dick Clark's television show, American Band Stand. Called *The Twist*:

Come on, baby, let's do the twist
Come on, baby, let's do the twist
Take me by my little hand and go like this.

This 1960 Chubby Checker song became a worldwide dancing sensation and sold more songs than Bing Crosby's White Christmas. I heard someone say.

"The rules of the senior-only *Fun Run* are simple. Jog *ten laps* around this four-hundred-and-forty-yard cinder track. You will finish here at this white finish pole.' He pointed. "Make me proud, you sons of Melville."

 Paul Henri, Ronnie Dudiak, and Captain Paul Henri took a deep breath and exhaled deeply in preparation for the fun run, and I, and the rest of the tryouts, quickly did the same.

We broke on Clark's three words: ready, set, and go. Captain Paul Henri bolted out in front of the pack, eager to show his *warrior ethos. I suspected all the Melville veterans took their place up front behind Captain Henri to feed their egos and look good in Coach Jim Clark's eyes.*

But Lax and I jogged happily and slowly along near the end of the pack, talking about everything and nothing.

"Look, the Melville fans and the Royals are starting to arrive, Natural," Lax said.

"Hey, Lax?"

"Yeah, Natural."

"I want to know one thing?"

"What one thing, Natural?"

"Why do you call me, Natural, Lax? Since Johnson Height's elementary school, you called me, Natural. Why?"

"I will tell you the answer to that important question before *you die* or after the last play of the last game. Whichever comes first?"

"Why does everyone around here talk about dying and death? We have our whole life ahead of us, don't we?"

"We absolutely do. Look at them all, Natural. Melville's finest, which isn't saying a lot."

Lax pointed to the stands. My eyes followed. I saw Bret Hart, the tryouts, the townies, the locals, the faithful, the partisans, the loyal, the face painters, the alumni, the football club, the mothers club, the booster club, and those fellows who never played football who Lax called the *Wannabes* and the *Never Where's* entering the stadium. The rest stood near Coach Clark.

"What is a *Wannabe Lax?*"

"Someone who wanted to be a Melville football player but never became one, but they wannabe one, that's a wannabe."

"Why do all these Melville sports fans come here today, Lax?"

"Which one's Natural?"

"All these Melville people. We have quite a cross-section of the town populous represented here today, you know."

"Some are here to see if Henri can win the Fun Run for the fourth year in a row, I suppose. Some come to watch what Bret Hart dubbed *Clark's Hell*. Others come to see Clark's keeper squad, the dirty thirty. They rest come for a host of unknown reasons."

"Hey, Lax."

"Yes, Natural?"

"Guess what I just saw."

"What did you just *see, Natural*, a log?"

"No! Fatso Hurst, the President of the Booster Club, just bet Frank Christian, the Melville football club president, two Ben Franklins that Captain Henri *won't win* this year's senior Fun Run."

"Are you sure, Natural?"

"Yes. They spat on their palms and shook on it."

"In Melville, that seals the deal, as horse traders did. When a man hand shakes hands and gives his word, his word is his bond.

"Do you think Captain Henri will win this year's Fun Run to Nowhere, Lax?"

"That depends, Natural. The conventional betting wisdom, of course, is that Henri will win again this year and by a very wide margin. But you can't count Bobby Hanuman or Ronnie Dudiak out just yet. All of these guys are fierce competitors. They are coming into their own. A cocky athlete filled with confidence is difficult to beat. They have super large egos to feed, and their pride is on the line. I think everyone is looking for validation at this age, Natural."

"You said Captain Henri has won this *Fun Run to Nowhere* in the last three years, right?"

"Yes, Henri lays it all down, full throttle. He puts the pedal to the metal and the rubber to the road. He is fearless."

"Oh my?"

"Oh my, I know what your oh my means. What is it now, Natural?"

"Well, Bobby Hanuman didn't get the memo about not passing Captain Henri.

"Bobby just passed the fearless cape crusader, Captain Paul Henri."

"Yep."

"There will be bloody hell to pay, and Bobby knows it. Henri will *retaliate*. Henri doesn't like being passed. No one sane who wants to avoid a beating in a fistfight passes Captain Henri, no one."

When Melville's star quarterback Bobby Hanuman passed Captain Henri in the fun run, he challenged the leader of the pack, the top dog, the lead alpha Alaskan Iditarod sled dog. Apparently, something no one had ever done before.

Bobby strengthened his lead over Henri by several more yards in sheer defiance. Frank Christian used Clark's red bullhorn to say. "Bobby Hanuman, what do you think you're doing, son, slithering past Captain Henri like that from the rear? I'm talking to you! Bobby, are you listening? You uppity lock-kneed lot lizard, you need Captain Henri. Captain Henri protects you. Captain Henri blocks for you. Darn your ungrateful hide!"

"Frank Christian is surely being a little rough on Bobby. Doesn't Coach Clark care about that, Lax? To be an effective team leader, the quarterback has to be respected."

"Coach Clark cares, but he placates the clubbers. It's politics, you know, and Clark is a master politician. These two jerks always get a free get out of jail free pass because Clark needs their support. The clubs have many members, giving them power and influence.

"Lax, how is it you're so smart?"

"Borderline genius."

"That must, must be wonderful."

"No, it's a curse."

"Why is Bobby hugging the inside lane."

"The inside lane is the shortest distance to run around this oval track. It saves him steps, naturally. I believe Bobby is serious about winning this thing."

I moved quickly to the inside lane.

"Bobby is stepping it up, Lax. He's extended his lead to fifteen yards now." Bobby strengthened his lead over Henri by several more yards in sheer defiance.

"Bobby's saying, *look at me. There is a new sheriff in town.*

Clark used the bullhorn to say. "Don't burn yourselves out on this ten-lap Missouri waltz, lads. Remember Aesop's fable, 'The Tortoise and the Hare; the turtle wins the day by going slow and easy.

"Natural, Clark has that Tortoise and the Hare Story all wrong."

"What, why, Lax?"

"Because a Tortoise only moves about 0.30 feet per second, while a Hare travels at approximately 8.8 feet per second. Do the math. Speed wins races." Lax said, telling me more than I wanted to know.

Frank Christian nervously borrowed the red megaphone when Fatso objected vehemently.

"Coach Clark gave it to me first, Frank, remember? So, give it back!"

"Au contraire, Fatso, Coach Clark promised it to me first. You're acting *sophomoric again,* Fatso."

"Now quit calling me *sophomoric,* Frank. You know that jacks my jaws. You know darn well I finished my junior year before I quit high school."

Fatso spoke with a stutter which got worse when he was frustrated and angry

"These two guys are a real piece of work. They both fight like two-grade school children in a sandbox, Lax not wanting the other to take full control of that red bullhorn."

Frank finally tired and handed the red bullhorn to Fatso.

Lax called them '*the wolf pack*' because they usually attacked in a pack. Lax said I should keep both my trained eyes and ears on them both. Which I did, and this is what I saw.

Most everyone in Melville knew why Fatso had quit high school as a junior to go to work at the Budweiser brewery in Saint Louis. Fatso fooled around, got his high school sweetheart in trouble, and had to get a job to support her and his new family. Everyone talked about it behind his back. Melville was funny that way. If they knew the smelly dirt, they would eagerly spread it around so everyone could smell it and then call it fertilizer.

Lax and I jogged easily, not yet caught up in the competitive moment, but things changed quickly on lap ten, the final lap. Henri took the lead back once again.

"It's very exciting to watch this competition from back here, in the rear of the pack, where the running is easier, huh, Lax?"

"Yes, but being last has its drawbacks, Natural."

"Like what, Lax?"

"Like not being in action, like letting someone else take all the glory when we both know they are not the best runners out here today."

"And?"

"Like being thought a loser. Lookie here, Natural, no more announcing; I have my pride too. I also have my image to uphold. I'm tired of being last here in the rear of the pack. Let's pass their rumps, Natural. Let's show them and Coach Clark and all the Melville whackos we have pride too. Let's give them their money's worth. Let's give them a show. No more, Mr. nice guys. Let the war games begin."

So we speeded up on the start of the crucial last lap for a beautiful late rally, coming from the rear, which I thought was a lot of fun and very exciting. The underdog always has a special place in America's heart.

CHAPTER TWELVE
WHERE YOUR HEAD GOES

"This is good racing fun, huh, Lax? I see why Bret Hart calls this the Fun Run to Nowhere. I love a good fast-paced foot race. Did I tell you? I was top dog in the fifth-grade May Day foot races at Johnson Heights Elementary School but not the sixth-grade race?"

"Oh, only about a thousand times, Natural. You do have a tendency to repeat yourself, you know. But why didn't you win the sixth-grade footrace? Natural, I forgot?"

"I got injured on the monkey bars."

"You were injured; how?"

"I reached too high."

"A monkey never leaves one branch without having another to hold on to."

"Should we pass Ronnie and then Bobby next, Lax?"

"Sure, why not?"

We drove our fresh speedy legs toward Ronnie and Bobby, and it felt good. Unfortunately, both Ronnie and Bobby tried to trip us as we ran past them. Lax, however, expected this bad behavior and quickly jumped over Ronnie's and Bobby's outstretched legs. I wasn't as lucky, but Lax slowed, turned, and quickly caught me and kept me from falling head-first on the cinder track.

"Stay up here with me, Natural, where it is safer, and I can keep an eye out for you. The hard slog is yet to come!"

"Should we pass Captain Henri next, Lax?"

"Sure, why not?"

"Maybe we should run behind him. Second is good."

"Second is never good. Second means you're not the best. The silver medal, not the gold medal, is never the best. No one remembers second-place finishers, do they?"

"Henri does."

We soon caught up to Captain Henri and started to pass him on the fourth curve.

"What are you two doing? Coming up on me fast from the rear? Trying to make me look bad? I'll rip both your hearts out and make you eat them if you try to pass me, Exley. You and the band boy will tire out, and then you'll drop out. Henri said, with his chin thrust out.

"How do we know if we are doing well, Lax?" I said breathlessly.

"When the lead Iditarod sled dog is barking at your heels, you know you are the pack's leader."

"Do you know what would bother me the most, Lax, if I were an Iditarod sled dog and not the pack's leader?"

"No, what, Natural?'

"The penthouse views!"

Lax smiled broadly.

"Yes, I see, but once you are number one, it's a better view."

"Catch us if you can, Henri," Lax said, taunting and purposely inciting Captain Henri, who snarled.

"You'll both be sorry in tackling practice and the bull in the ring later in practice."

"And what does Henri have that is so special, Lax?"

"Henri, that boy is a mechanized machine; he won't quit."

Frank Christian pulled the red bull horn from Fatso's tightly clutched fists and said.

"Ok, ok, it's your turn now, Henri. Show us what you got. Get here any way you can. Just get here first, Henri. Henri, do you hear me?"

My brother Tom once said:

"The prideful ego works in strange and mysterious ways.

If you do not come out on top,

Accept defeat without being defeated."

"I knew you two pond toads couldn't hold that bristling pace to the finish line. Exley, you and the *band boy* are finished now and forever, and you both know it."

Henri, spurred on by the hopeful Frank Christian, passed both Lax and me fifty yards out from the finish line.

What I knew was this. Not to be outdone, Lax Exley pushed the pedal to the metal of his 1958 retractable hardtop *Ford Sky liner* with that four-barrel 352 V-8 300 HP interceptor engine. This action put his engine into its *kick-down gear,* a gear designed for extra power and a fresh burst of speed.

When the gas hit the carburetor, it passed into the engine cylinder blocks and quickly combusted. Lax shivered, shook, and then lurched forward with a jerk and two quick jolts. Lax drove his two-toned cream and sky blue fifty-eight Ford muscle car toward the finish pole with a wild, bold dash in an attempt to pass Captain Henri.

Upon seeing Lax Exley's last-ditch heroic effort and being touched by his determination and strong will and these words,

"Now or never kick it, Natural, kick it!"

I settled in behind Lax.

Henri's arms began flailing, his form going south as we passed him. Finally, Henri turned and snarled like a wounded animal.

"I'll rip both your throats out with my own two hands."

It seems nothing is a better motivator for young men than to be verbally challenged in front of others.

Now smelling a glorious victory, fatso jumped up and down as if on a pogo stick.

My mind blurred at this time but placing fear against hope. I sprinted with all I had left. If life is a journey, that white finish pole was now my destination.

Fatso began to snap his fingers, matching each stride we four took toward that slim white finish pole.

I quickly learned, however, running all out full tilt makes your lungs sting and cry out loud for air and mercy, and you tire very quickly.

"That's it, bring it home like *Gang Busters*. Bring it home, fellows. Only fifteen yards to go for victory, boys." Fatso yelled.

Gang Buster's was a popular radio crime fighter show.

"You two *hooligans* have lost. You're both *losers*." Frank Christian yelled. "Give it up."

Lax didn't want to let Fatso down-one of his fiercest critics-go figure that. Lax gathered himself once more for this one final supreme effort. Lax pulled it from only God knows where and I followed him.

What happened next surprised and shocked everyone.

My brother Tom says:

Where your head goes, your body is sure to follow.

Some people claim Lax simply came undone. But I felt he had merely lost his form and then his balance and purposely went sprawling across the finish line head first while others vehemently disagreed. Lax went down hard and fast, landing hard on his face and knees on the cinder track. His head crossed the finish line for my money first, followed by his body.

Frank turned quickly and asked Clark anxiously.

"Who won, coach?"

Clark looked startled. He slowly removed his red Melville cap, wiped the sweat from his broad forehead with the palm of his hand, withdrew a few steps, and splattered the perspiration down on the field with the flip of his wrist. Then, looking puzzled, Clark did not answer Frank.

So, Frank asked Clark again.

"Who won, Coach, Henri?"

"Well, Frank, it looked that way at first light. It was a magnificent run, his best ever, I think, because he was pushed."

"But Henri won, of course, Coach, just like he did last year and the year before that, right?" Frank said.

To my surprise coach, Clark would not answer Frank directly.

Fatso stepped forward quickly.

"It was one big blur, huh, Coach? But Lax *Exley* won easily, right, *Exley* was first, and the *band boy* took second, right Coach?"

"Not so fast, Fatso, not so fast. I don't think we...."

"But Exley clearly won, right Coach? I mean in a final spurt, in a final spurt." Fatso said.

"You saw it best, Coach. You saw it best." Frank Christian said.

"Yes, I saw it best from my vantage point at the finishing pole, and I have crystal clear vision, but I'm not sure what I saw. I never saw a foot race so close, never! It was the dandiest thing I ever saw, a photo finish. We needed a speed camera, like the one they use at the Melville race track. What would one of those high-priced cameras cost you, fellows, to purchase?"

I ran over to Lax, breathing heavily. I helped Lax to his feet.

"Thanks, buddy, I needed that," Lax said.

Fatso turned abruptly and quickly walked over to congratulate Lax. Fatso used what salespeople call the *assumed close*. Something Fatso learned from being a part-time insurance salesman, no doubt. Fatso slapped Lax Exley on his back, shook his hand vigorously, and spoke loudly like some people do when they want to get their way.

"Wow, you sure laid the rubber down, Lax," Fatso said.

"A huh."

"You blew out your left tennis shoe, I see."

"Yeah, I blew out the left front toe, Fatso, see. I wore my magical Buster Brown Froggie and the magic twanger tennis shoes."

"You fell down, huh?"

"Ah huh."

"Did you throw yourself across the finish line on purpose?"

"Ah huh, I had to!

"You flew through the air."

"Ah, huh, I thought I could fly."

I knew you could do it. I knew it all the time. How does your split lip feel?"

"Ah, it feels swollen and stings a lot, but it was worth it."

"It's bleeding badly?"

"Yeah, ah huh!"

"It's what we in the band call *a fat lip*. How did you gather yourself for both of those final pushes, for that last supreme effort?" I asked.

"Well, I wanted to have some fun, Natural. Whipping Henri, Ronnie, Bobby, and the boys is always fun. It's a football guy thing. We are all good friends and teammates, and I would die for them, but we all love outdoing the other. It's a football guy thing."

Lax possessed calm amid a storm.

"I thought I kicked it in way too early, Natural. I thought I might fizzle out. But once in the air, I couldn't catch myself from falling. I thought it was over when Henri rallied and charged with the sheer determination of a wild grizzly bear. Lax said.

"It looked difficult, Lax."

"Nay, it wasn't that hard, Natural. You dance the hokey pokey, and you turn yourself around. I got my second wind, look, I'm not even breathing hard, see, oh yeah, I had a peaceful easy feeling back there, and I'm standing strong now. See, legs aren't wobbling, like yours are Natural, and I feel great."

Lax split his upper and lower lips when he fell on the track. His nose began to bleed and covered his practice jersey. The black cinders were embedded solidly in both his knees and elbows. Some blood came there. All for what I wondered. To get his rightful share of the Fun Run to Nowhere *glory*. It seemed silly to me but not to Lax. But after closer inspection, it was clear this race took a toll on his body. This, in my mind, made Lax the loser and not the winner. But then, maybe I did not understand all that was at stake.

Clark walked over and stood beside Lax.

"Laxly, what happened here? Give me your take. Do you think you whipped Henri and the boys?"

"Well, if I won the fun run, it was because it was in my *karma* to win, Coach."

Henri quickly walked up behind Lax, punched him twice in the right kidney, and put poor Lax in a deadly choke hold.

"And now it is in my Karma to kick your backside, Exley."

"Now, Henri, Fair is fair," Clark said strongly.

Henri released Lax from his choke hold and shoved him to the cinder track hard.

Embarrassed, Lax chuckled. Then he stood slowly.

"Exley won, right Coach?" Fatso said, moving closer.

Clark removed his cap and scratched his head again and again. Clark shook his head up and down and then sideways, not giving Frank or Fatso a definitive answer.

Since no one in authority would make the crucial call, I did.

"Lax Exley won by a head, Coach."

"What, are you sure, Cameron? Who was second?'

"Bobby was third. Henri was forth. Ronnie Dudiak was fifth. Big John was sixth. Then Serge, Willis, Dave, and Bechtel finished last."

"Holy Mother, full of grace, Henri finished in fourth place!" Fatso said loudly. Captain Henri spoke up in his defense quickly.

"Don't listen to the band, boy, Coach. No one can beat Henri, right? You know that's the truth, don't you Coach?' Captain Henri said.

"Yes, but hold on, Henri. The band boy had a different perspective. Don't dismiss the band boy quite so fast. He was there; he could see the winner."

"Paul Henri never runs second. Paul Henri has never lost. Paul Henri is undefeated, three years straight."

Captain Henri referred to himself in the third person.

"You see, that's just it; that's the thing, Henri. This year's Fun Run defies imagination; they passed you, then you passed them, then they passed again. Finally, they came flying by; it was just like *thunder,* you could *hear it,* but you couldn't *see it*. Then Exley blew out his left tennis shoe at the finish pole, and he started falling, his arms flailing. My eyes followed him. He flew across the finish line head first. Ass over tin cups and fell hard on his face. He busted his lips. The hard fall will place a black tattoo from the embedded cinders on both his knees." Coach Clark said.

Frank Christian placed his arm around the left shoulder of Coach Clark as if they were school chums and old friends.

"Here is the main thing we need to know. Did Exley and the band boy win this race, or did last year's winner Henri, win again this year? I think we all know the answer to that question. Henri won easily by a nose; there is no hiding that fact." Frank said.

Fatso spoke up quickly.

"No, no, no. According to the band boy, Henri apparently ran out of gas Frank and *finished fourth without apologizing*. So don't apologize for picking the true winner. It was Exley, we all know that Exley who won this year's fun run. So right coach, Exley won?"

Now Clark was in a preverbal pickle. Clark had to choose between the football clubbers and the booster clubbers; men from both of these clubs helped make his football program great. Clark removed his Melville cap once again and held it in both hands. He wiped his brow. Then his face lit up. It was a Harry Truman moment.

"You can't be too hasty, fellows. Let the dust clear. Let it settle. Don't act so brash. Do you fellows remember when the Chicago Tribune got the *1948 presidential election* result all wrong? The headline read:

'Dewey defeats Truman.'

"That call put an egg on the Tribune's face."

"But the Exley won, Coach, right? Exley won?" Fatso said.

"We are seeking the truth here, fellows. It's my call."

"Yes, it is your call, Coach. You saw it best, Coach. Don't let me influence you. But somebody had to win." Fatso said, pressing his point.

"Henri has never lost, never lost," Frank said. "Now that's the truth and one fact you can trust and believe in."

Clark tried to skate his way out of it. Determining who won this race seemed harder than stuffing lightning in a jar. And so, it went back and forth. Did Iax whip Captain Henri and the boys, or did Henri, Bobby, or Ronnie Dudiak take the blue ribbon that day?

"If you had to pick a winner, coach, you had to pick a winner, who would it be, my boy Henri or Exley?" Frank said.

"If I had to pick a winner, Frank, I would do so begrudgingly, but I think Exley put an egg on all our faces today."

"Then Exley won?"

"Yes, Frank. Exley put on a last-ditch effort like none I have ever seen. He pulled from God knows where and won the race, diving past the finish line. So here it is, fellows. No more talking, no more fading to black.

Finally, hearing Clark's decision brought a tear of joy to my eyes, rolling down my cheek and washing my face. Then, realizing where I was, I turned away so no one could see my little bitty tear.

"Is that your final answer, Coach?" Fatso asked. "Exley won."

"Yes, I believe it is Fatso; I believe it is."

Frank Christian, upon hearing that Henri had lost, turned and faced Captain Henri angrily.

"You let Exley and the band boy beat you, Henri. How could you do this to me? You have never lost this race in the last three years, Henri. You have never been beaten, and now you are beaten by Exley and a dam green pea rookie. That is reprehensible? What have you got to say for yourself Henri?"

"I started out too fast, Frank. They came by me out of nowhere."

"It's not how you start out; it is how you finish," Frank said. "Fatso and his minions are dancing happily; look at them."

"They surprised me, Frank. They came out from somewhere in the rear. I never expected the sudden surge. I looked back. I lost my stride. They bumped me. You saw at. It was *unforgettable and regrettable,* Frank. I ran after them twice like a wild man! They both ran inside of me, jostled, and nipped me at the pole in a final gallant surge. They had guts; you gotta give em that. They had guts. But did you see Exley throw himself through the air at the finish line? You got to admire that; he has guts."

"Guts hell, you didn't bust it bubble butt, you lump of bituminous coal." Even Bobby and Ronnie Dudiak and the band boy beat you. Fourth place. How could this happen to us, Henri? This was to be our finest hour, another glorious moment, winning the fun run four years in a row, and you bungled it, Henri, unbelievable, unbelievable?"

Frank fumed, chided, and scolded Henri for several minutes, still not believing or accepting the result-while. Fatso pranced around the track like one of those stunningly beautiful white Arabian parade horses in the Barnum and Bailey circus.

Fatso was now pleased as punch, and with our winning performance, he tucked two hundred dollars neatly in his back pocket and smiled. He danced around on one leg in merriment, and I had his one moment in time, never to be forgotten.

And so, it happened; we had no definitive answer. Fatso won his bet, and Frank quickly slipped two hundred dollars into Fatso's back pocket, wrapped tighter than a Cuban cigar so Clark could not see.

Jim Clark glanced down at his gold wrist watch indicating this initial phase of our training was over. He placed his whistle to his mouth with his right hand. Clarks' golden whistle sounded loud and everyone lined up on the black cinder track, ready to run *Clark's hell*.

Made in United States
Orlando, FL
24 March 2023